Magnolias and murder—live oaks and dead women—romance and violence—are what three unsuspecting women find on the Garden Club Pilgrimage to glamorous old Natchez. Expecting to recapture the magic of the Old South, they become involved, instead, in an ancient feud of love and death, where the romantic sins of the past come to life in very modern murder.

Persons in the *Mystery*

·"Murder With Southern Hospitality"

LOUISE GOULD,
whose husband warned her against going to Natchez on the annual Garden Club Pilgrimage, begins the trip as an innocent passenger —with misgivings—and almost ends it as a corpse.

CORNELIA CARTWRIGHT,
President of the Brentwood Garden Club, has a six-corsage bosom and a way of taking all opposition as a personal matter. She is perfectly capable of presiding over any—almost any—situation; and Louise Gould is certain that Cornelia will receive next to Saint Peter at the Pearly Gates.

MISS LETTY DRAYTON,
born to be secretary and maid-of-all-work of any club she belongs to, seems completely dominated by Cornelia. She is a gentle, sweet-faced little mouse of a woman, but she can change into a savage tiger-cat if she's pushed far enough.

STEVE HEYWOOD,
who doesn't know a garden from third base, does know that when he marries he'll pick out the girl all by himself.

MR. ED (JUDGE) DRAYTON,
Miss Letty's brother and present master of Antigua, the family home, is a cold, steely man. If he has ever smiled, there is no memory of it left in his face.

ANNE DRAYTON,
Miss Letty's niece, has eyes dark like Mr. Ed's but soft like Miss Letty's. She is willing to please her uncle rather than herself by marrying the man he has chosen for her.

(Continued on next page)

Persons in the *Mystery*
"Murder With Southern Hospitality"

(Continued from preceding page)

LAWRENCE DRAYTON,
Mr. Ed's son, is a younger edition of his father, but he has a down-the-nose air toward the visiting Pilgrims which contradicts the tradition about hospitality in the Old South.

MISS KATE DRAYTON,
Miss Letty's sister, is cast in the same mold, though with harsher lines than her brother Mr. Ed. Her ill health confines her to Antigua, and she doesn't hide her bitterness toward Miss Letty.

ALEC CARTWRIGHT,
good-looking in a blond, clean-cut way, is Cornelia's stepson. He provides both an unnecessary complication and an easy way out for Anne Drayton in her romantic dilemma.

LUSBY,
Cornelia's colored chauffeur, wants nothing to do with the gun she always keeps in the glove compartment—he says.

MILLICENT STORM and CORA JOHNSON,
friends of Cornelia's and fellow Pilgrims, are well-fed and well-corseted ladies with smartly coiffed white hair, rouge a little too pink and powder a little too white. They've met Cornelia before on tours, and Millicent never forgets a face.

ISAAC,
butler of Antigua, has kinky hair which is as white as frost and a toothless grin. He hopes Miss Letty has come home to stay.

COUSIN ROSE,
called by Pilgrims a "quaint old chatelaine," makes ends meet by renting rooms at Tangiers, her ancestral home.

JIM BAILEY,
sheriff, is more than baffled—he is stumped—by the maniac who goes around murdering visiting club women. It's bad for Natchez's reputation, and the murders are a civic problem.

DOCTOR RICHARDS,
brisk and businesslike, is quite nice about being routed out of bed at any time of night to tie up arteries.

MURDER WITH SOUTHERN HOSPITALITY

By LESLIE FORD

Author of "The Woman in Black,"
"The Philadelphia Murder Story,"
"The Devil's Stronghold," etc.

WILDSIDE PRESS

Murder with Southern Hospitality

Published by Wildside Press LLC
wildsidepress.com

MURDER WITH SOUTHERN HOSPITALITY

List of *Exciting* Chapters—

Murder With Southern Hospitality

Chapter One

JOURNEY WITH FOREBODINGS

I DON'T KNOW WHAT would happen if women started taking
their husbands' advice, but I know what wouldn't have
happened if I'd taken Tom's. I wouldn't have gone to
Natchez for the Garden Club Pilgrimage, not with Cornelia Cartwright and Letty Drayton, anyway. I wouldn't,
moreover, have had my picture in every newspaper in the
country as friend of the murdered club woman. Nor would
I have had to explain the headlines *Doctor's Wife Reveals
Hidden Love* to everybody who assumed it was *my* hidden
love—including, for one pretty uncomfortable moment,
Tom himself. It did have one advantage, however. Everybody in town developed sudden and inexplicable ail-
ments and rushed to the office, so that we're putting the
new wing on the house this year instead of next. All things
being equal, I think we'd rather have waited.

Even before Tom said, "You must be losing your mind,
old girl," I'd begun to have very definite misgivings of my
own. It was at a meeting of the State Council of Federated
Garden Clubs. The vice-president had been to Natchez
and was showing us the movies she'd taken. Cornelia Cartwright, who's president and has what somebody irreverent-
ly called a six-corsage bosom, said she thought we all ought
to go to Natchez just to see what a group of women with
real civic determination could do when they put their
minds to it. Of course none of us had to go to Natchez to
see that. All we had to do was look at Cornelia. And a little
later when Cornelia said she thought she'd go herself, and
take a couple of friends along to share expenses, it didn't

occur to any one that Letty Drayton would be one of them
—least of all to Miss Letty herself.

I've always wanted to see Natchez, so when Cornelia
asked me to go I said I'd love to.

"It won't cost us very much," she said practically. Being
the widow of a little man who made a million and a half
in fertilizer and died leaving it to her quite intact, Cornelia's petty economies are sometimes a little hard to take,
though not as hard for her friends as for Alec Cartwright,
her deceased husband's son by a former marriage. "And I
think, my dear," she went on, "I'll take Letty. She comes
from Natchez. It'll be a treat for her, the poor thing, and
we can stay with her people. She has a brother and a sister
still living in the family house. I'll just speak to her now."

I glanced across Cornelia's expensively decorated drawing-room to where Miss Letty was mopping up the loose
ends of the day's business and getting her books and corre-
spondence in order. Miss Letty had been born to be the secretary and maid-of-all-work of any club she belonged to,
just as Cornelia Cartwright had been born to be its president. She looked like a dusty little sparrow, molting slightly, in a whole aviary of opulently plumed and opulently
fed pouter pigeons, all chattering shrilly over tea and sandwiches and tiny iced cakes that aren't *really* fattening, my
dear, unless you eat a *great* many. Miss Letty never got
around to eating until the sandwiches were a few dog-
eared, slightly soggy remnants and the tea was cold, con-
centrated poison. But she never seemed to mind. She
looked up at Cornelia bearing down on her now like a
Spanish galleon in full rigging and smiled expectantly.

"I've decided to go to Natchez, Letty," Cornelia said.

"You'll love it, Cornelia," Miss Letty said. "The pictures made me just as homesick as anything." She picked
up the Natchez Garden Club folder in front of her and
looked at it wistfully. A woman standing beside the table
turned and said, "You come from Natchez, don't you? Is

your home on the tour?"

"Oh, no," Miss Letty answered quickly.

"It's just the mansions they show to visitors," Cornelia said.

"I suppose so." The woman turned away and went on talking.

Miss Letty put the folder down. "I'm sure you'll enjoy it, Cornelia."

"I'm going to take you along," Cornelia Cartwright said.

Miss Letty looked up with something more like alarm than the joyful surprise that Cornelia's tone seemed to expect to elicit.

"Oh, no," she said quickly. "That's awfully nice of you, but I can't. I really can't."

"Nonsense," Cornelia said. "It'll do you good to get away. I'll pay your expenses."

I still don't quite know how she made a very generous offer—if you know Cornelia—sound so appallingly patronizing. Miss Letty flushed.

"That's very kind of you, Cornelia," she said. "But I couldn't accept it, really I couldn't. Thank you just the same."

Cornelia Cartwright flushed too. "You're just being silly, Letty," she said, rather sharply. "I should think you'd be delighted to have the opportunity of seeing your family and your old home again."

Miss Letty's flush deepened almost painfully.

"Of course I would, Cornelia. But—"

"Then that settles it. You're going along."

Cornelia turned back to the guests whose cars were moving up in the driveway to take them home. "I must say it's very hard to do nice things for some people," she said, and Miss Letty, who couldn't have helped hearing her, blinked a little and shook her head to the maid holding out a silver tray with two little cakes rather the worse for wear on it. She got up and gathered her books and papers together, so distressed—out of all proportion to what had happened —that I felt very sorry for her. When she went up the stairs I slipped out as soon as I could and followed her.

She wasn't in the blue guest room, but I knew she hadn't gone. Her ratty old Hudson seal coat was still on the bed, pathetic and out of place among the glossy black Persian lambs and lustrous minks around it. I've known Miss Letty since my husband came to town to practise medicine five years ago, and her coat was old even then.

I went across the hall and opened the door of Cornelia's Williamsburg apricot guest room. Miss Letty was standing in front of the window, dabbing at her eyes with a sodden handkerchief. She glanced around like a frightened rabbit, and looked relieved at seeing me—instead of Cornelia, I suppose.

"Don't be upset, Miss Letty," I said. "You know what Cornelia's like. She doesn't mean it, really. Don't let her browbeat you into going if you don't want to."

"It isn't that," she said wretchedly. "It's just that—well, I can't explain. I'd *like* to go. I haven't seen—I mean, I haven't been there for—for a long time. But I wouldn't want to embarrass—I mean, Cornelia would expect to—to stay with my family. She wouldn't understand—"

She hesitated again, pulling nervously at her handkerchief.

"I'll just have to tell Cornelia I can't afford to go, and can't allow her to pay my way."

"But we're driving down, Miss Letty," I said. "It can't cost Cornelia very much."

"Are you going too?"

I nodded.

She hesitated still, her gentle eyes searching mine.

"No—I can't," she said. "I really can't. I just haven't got the money."

I had more than a vague feeling even then that it wasn't only the money. I could understand easily enough why she didn't want to be under that kind of an obligation to Cornelia Cartwright. It would mean she could never call her vote her own again, because Cornelia had a way of taking opposition as a personal matter. On the other hand, she so completely dominated Miss Letty already that it didn't seem to matter much. It wasn't, however, until after our local club meeting two weeks later that the feeling I'd had watching her fumble with her sodden handkerchief became a definite conviction.

If Cornelia hadn't invited Miss Letty to go in front of the State Council, I'm sure she'd have let the whole thing drop. There were plenty of people who'd have loved to go, and as Cornelia said very forcibly, she was just trying to do the poor thing a favor. Things being as they were, it passed abruptly from a favor to a challenge, and Cornelia was never a woman to make a challenge without getting the best of it. Miss Letty was going to Natchez if she had to be carried there bound and gagged. I'd seen that in Cornelia's eye as Miss Letty and I left her house two weeks before, and at our meeting she took the chair with the kind of grim determination she normally used only when the city fathers were about to allow a tree to be cut down at the foot of Main Street. The result was that the Club passed a resolution of thanks to Miss Letty for her ten years' work as secretary and voted fifty dollars to pay her expenses to the Natchez Garden Club Pilgrimage, with the request that she read a paper about it at the May meeting. There were two dissenting votes, Miss Letty's and mine. I voted against it because I saw something in her face that made me acutely and heartbreakingly aware that there was really some other reason for her not wanting to go back to Natchez.

She seemed to me all of a sudden like some harmless little creature beating against invisible bars, and when everybody was so touched by the tears in her eyes when she stammered out her thanks I could have shaken them. The tears were there, but they were tears of defeat; her protests that the Club could use the money to finish the planting around the Memorial Cross were brushed aside, for the kindest possible reason that everybody really wanted to do something nice for poor Miss Letty.

She sat down, her hands folded in her lap to keep them from trembling, her face quite pale, the tears still beading her eyelashes and running in little furrows out of the corners of her eyes. Everybody else was pleased and happy and laughing at her for being so silly and sweet about it. She was still trembling so, when I helped her on with her coat, that her hand got stuck in the worn lining.

"Whatever will I do?" she whispered shakily. "I'll have to go now."

"Don't if you don't want to," I said.

"But everybody would think it was awful, if I didn't. There's no way I could explain. I'll write to my family."

She took hold of my hand, her own quite cold.

"Please try to explain to Cornelia that we'll be more comfortable at the hotel—will you, Louise?"

I did, and I got about as far with it as I'd thought I would.

"I told Letty frankly I thought it would look peculiar, to say the least, if we went down there and put up at a hotel," Cornelia said flatly. "Nobody expects Letty's family to live in the lap of luxury. I've no doubt we'll be very uncomfortable indeed, but for the looks of the thing *here*— not there—we'll just have to put up with it. We both understand that a great many very nice people in the South are very poor. I think it's the duty of friendship to put up with that sort of thing in order to show the people down there that Letty's friends are above that kind of snobbery. If you think you're too good to stay with Letty's people, Louise, you can stop at the hotel. I'm certainly very much surprised at you, is all I can say, my dear."

I knew it was useless to try to protest. Staying at Miss

Letty's had started out to be a saving of our lodging rent. Cornelia had forgotten that.

She came to the door with me as I was leaving.

"You know, Louise," she said—I saw the parallel lines between her brows deepen—"maybe I shouldn't mention it, but it may be what you have in mind. I've heard about some old families in the South going terribly to seed, and living in old houses without even what we regard as the necessities of decent living, and I don't mean bathtubs, or chickens running in and out. I wonder— I mean, you don't suppose—"

"I don't know," I said. "I think we'd better stay at the hotel."

When Tom kissed me good-by the morning we left he said, "Remember—if the going gets too tough, send me an SOS and I'll wire you to come home, I've eaten ground glass." He grinned. "It won't be the first time. And you'd better take this—you may need it." He stuffed an extra wad of bills into my bag. "So long, angel. You brought it on yourself."

It wasn't until we got to Nashville, Tennessee, that I began to have any very serious misgivings again. I'd got quite used to arriving in places around five o'clock and waiting unblushingly in the car with Miss Letty while Cornelia, having consulted her address book, called up and got all three of us—and Lusby her colored chauffeur—invited to dine and spend the night with people she'd met at conventions. So far all the trip had cost any of us was gas and oil, hamburgers one day when Cornelia didn't know anybody in that county in East Tennessee, and two toothbrushes for Miss Letty. She was always forgetting her toothbrush. In Nashville we stopped to get her a third one, and Cornelia said to me, "I haven't told you, but we are stopping with Letty's family. She finally wrote to them and they said we mustn't think of going to the hotel. I've told her frankly I think it's very wrong of her to be ashamed of them. She's so spineless. She really irritates me beyond endurance."

"I don't think she's spineless," I said. "I think she's just a very gentle, unselfish human being who lets herself be put upon by everybody."

"That's spineless," Cornelia said.

But both of us were wrong, it seemed. That night we'd left our hostess, whom Cornelia had met at a D.A.R. convention in Washington once, and had gone upstairs to bed. Miss Letty and I were sharing a room. She was in the bathroom undressing when Cornelia came in, her face covered with cold cream, her hair in a pink net to keep the waves flat. She went over to the dressing-table and wiped her fingers on a piece of tissue, looking down at the gold Victorian locket that Miss Letty always wore on a black satin ribbon around her neck. She picked it up.

"I wish Letty would sell this to me," she said.

She wasn't the only one who wished that. It was really lovely. The back was delicately chased arabesque, and on the face was a spray of lilies of the valley tied with a bowknot of rubies. The stem and green leaves were tiny encrusted emeralds, the bells pearls. It always looked a little out of place on Miss Letty, people said who wanted it— and she *does* need the money, my dear.

"What do you suppose is in it?" Cornelia asked. She started to open it at just the moment that the bathroom door opened. For an instant Miss Letty stood stock-still, staring at Cornelia, pressing at the catch. Then she sprang forward, just as the two halves broke open and a tiny bit of paper fell to the floor. Her eyes were blazing with anger as she wrenched it out of Cornelia's astonished hands.

"Don't you dare!" she cried.

Cornelia stood completely aghast, too appalled to say a word.

"Where is it?" Miss Letty cried. "The paper that was in it!"

"It's on the floor, Miss Letty,'" I said.

She looked down frantically, bent down and seized it, her breath coming in quick gasps. She held the locket tightly to her flannel dressing-gown, still facing Cornelia, her face white with anger.

"Don't you ever dare touch that again!" she cried passionately.

Cornelia literally sagged under the attack.

"I'm sorry, Letty," she stammered. "I didn't mean to offend you. I didn't—"

She drew herself up again. "If you'll excuse me, I think I'll go back to my room."

"I think I'll wash my face," I said, and went into the bathroom.

When I came out, Miss Letty was in bed, lying perfectly still, her eyes closed. I could see a bit of black ribbon sticking out from under her pillow. I put up the windows and turned out the lights. The piece of paper that had suddenly transformed a gentle sweet-faced little mouse of a woman into something as dynamic and savage as a tiger-cat was indelibly fixed on my retina even in the dark. It was about half an inch wide and folded so that it was about an inch long. It looked like a clipping from a newspaper column, and old, because it was faded a yellowish-gray as I'd seen it on the white rug under the dressing-table.

It took me a long time to go to sleep that night.

Chapter Two

STRANGE CAR FOLLOWING

WHETHER MISS LETTY had made her peace with Cornelia
Cartwright while I was taking my bath, or they'd both decided to ignore the incident, I don't know. At any rate, we
started out the next morning as serenely—outwardly—as
if nothing had occurred at all. Miss Letty was wearing her
locket as usual. If it seemed to me that every time I happened to glance at Cornelia she was looking at it covertly,
out of one corner of her eyes, I have to admit that I was
making a definite effort not to do the same thing. There
was something about the set of Cornelia's mouth, however,
that indicated she was by no means through with the matter—not yet. Miss Letty sat between us in the back seat of
the big car, not saying very much and not always hearing
what was said to her.

"Now this is *very* interesting," Cornelia announced.

We'd come, the road sign said, into the old Natchez
Trace—the historic route of Indians, explorers, trappers,
pioneers, highwaymen, and tourists. Miss Letty's hand
went to her throat as if she suddenly had difficulty breath-
ing.

Cornelia looked at her sharply. "I should think you'd be
glad to be coming back here, Letty," she said severely.

"Oh, I am, really I am, in a way," Miss Letty said.

"Well, you certainly don't act it." There was a metallic
edge on Cornelia's voice.

I suppose you can't live with suppressed fear, in as close
quarters as Cornelia and I had been living, for three days
without its beginning to tell on you. I hadn't realized, however, how jittery we'd got until Cornelia glanced back
through the rear window and said abruptly, "Don't look

now, Louise, but isn't that the same car that's been following us ever since we left Richmond?"

She leaned forward, slid open the glass panel, and said, "Lusby—isn't that the car that's been following us? It's that same young man that was talking to you the other night, isn't it?"

The driver glanced into the mirror and grinned. "Yas'm, that's th' same one, Mis' Cartwright. He been right on our tail two days now."

I looked back, too. The straight road through banks of white dogwood was empty except for the old tan touring car that we'd first seen at a service station in Richmond, and later seen again going through the Smoky Mountains National Park. The young man at the wheel was the same young man, the battered gray felt hat pulled down almost to his ears, its brim rippling in the breeze, was the same battered gray felt hat.

"I must say," Cornelia said, "I don't like the looks of it. Why should he be following us this way, Lusby?"

"Don' you-all worry none," Lusby said cheerfully. "This here cah got mo' speed than that ol' bus ever reckoned of."

He went up to seventy-five without an effort.

"Now, Lusby," Cornelia said sharply. "I'd rather be robbed than die in a ditch. As soon as you get him out of sight you can slow down. We don't all want to be killed."

I looked back again at the old touring car plugging along at about forty-five, gradually receding in the distance.

"Maybe he's going to Natchez too," I said. "That would explain it quite simply. He looked to me like a very engaging young man."

"Explain it too simply, in my opinion," Cornelia retorted. " You can't go by looks, and anyway it's better to be safe than sorry. You can't tell what's going to happen to anybody, these days."

I smiled and shook my head. I suppose everybody goes through life not recognizing Truth when he hears it. I doubt if Cornelia herself had any idea of what a prophetic utterance she was making. In fact I'm sure she hadn't, because at the moment she was too busy unloosing the clasp of her diamond wrist watch. I watched her tuck it down into the ash receiver fitted into the broadcloth armrest beside her.

"You'd better put your locket in here too, Letty. You don't want it ripped off you. It's just the kind of thing they're looking for."

She leaned forward again. "Have you got that gun, Lusby?"

"Yas'm, Ah got it," Lusby said. "But Ah don't want nothin' to do with it, Mis' Cartwright. Ah don' want nothin' to do with no shootin'. But Ah got it, if that's what you're askin' me."

Cornelia slid the glass panel into place and settled back into her seat. She looked out the back window again.

"Well, anyway, we've lost him," she said. "He's not likely to catch up with us at this rate. You'd think they'd have a patrol on this road. If you see one, Louise, I'll stop him and report that car. After all, we're just three women in strange country, and I think it's better not to take any chances."

She spoke as though Mississippi were the interior of Indo-China and we were three meek and helpless moonflowers.

"Now if this is the town I think it is, there's a good place for lunch and an antique shop run by a woman I met at a convention in South Carolina last year."

I didn't go to the antique shop. As we came out of the lunchroom I saw the tan touring car with the young man in the battered felt hat pull up at a service station across the street. Cornelia's car was there too. I saw Lusby look around at the young man and grin, and look over to see if

Mrs. Cartwright had caught him in that treasonable act. Coming up the undistinguished main street was a state patrol car. My heart sank, but Cornelia had her sun glasses on and was also, thank heavens, looking the other way. Her diamond wrist watch, I remembered suddenly, was still in the ash receiver.

"I've got to go to the drug store," I said hurriedly. "I'll join you at the car."

I thought somebody ought to warn the young man before he found himself in jail. I went across the street. He was perched on the dusty fender of his ancient jalopy eating a hot dog. He certainly had none of the earmarks of a youthful criminal. His hat was pushed on the back of his sandy nondescript thatch of curly hair, his eyes were bright blue and twinkling, and his nose was peeling. He pulled off his hat and grinned.

"I'll bet you a Coke you're garden clubbers pilgrimaging to Natchez," he said.

"You win," I said.

He grinned again.

"That's my Quaker blood—I only bet on sure things. I knew it the minute I spotted the old gal with the pansies on her hat. She's the spit of my Aunt Selina. My Aunt Selina's covered more miles on pilgrimages than all the pilgrims of the Middle Ages."

He bent his head sideways and looked at me critically.

"Now you haven't been on many pilgrimages. You haven't got the professional air. It takes years to get it. Is the old gal *your* Aunt Selina?"

"No," I said. "She's just president of our Garden Club."

He grinned again.

"You didn't have to tell me that. I already told you she looks like my Aunt Selina."

"Well, anyway," I said. "You'd better be careful. She's going to have you arrested."

"Who, me?"·He didn't look at all dismayed. "What for?"

"Because you've been following us for two days."

He coughed up a piece of hot dog that had gone down his throat the wrong way and wiped the tears out of his eyes.

"That's because I'm too lazy to look at road maps," he said. "I just figured if I kept behind you, I'd get to Natchez sooner or later. I don't seem to be able to make you understand about my Aunt Selina."

"Is your Aunt Selina in Natchez?"

"No. She's taking a year off, doing South American gardens."

"Are you pinch-hitting for her down here?"

"Good Lord, no," he said. "I don't know a garden from third base. I'm on my way to Kelly Field. Just going through Natchez out of cussedness—or curiosity, I don't know which."

He started on his third hot dog. I'd never seen any one so completely at ease with himself and the world.

"You'd laugh if you knew why I'm going," he said. "It sounds crazy. It *is* crazy. My father came from Natchez. He had an old cousin down here. I only saw the old boy a couple of times, but when he died he left me half a dozen ratty plantations."

"That was very nice of him," I said.

"Yes, but there was a catch in it. To get 'em I had to marry a gal down here before I was twenty-six, or she'd get 'em instead of me."

"How old are you now?"

"Twenty-six in October," he said.

"You'd better hurry then, hadn't you?"

"Not on your life. I wrote and said, 'Dear Miss So-and-so, you can have the plantations, I've never drunk cotton gin but I don't think I'd like it,' or something to that effect. The lawyer wrote back and said I couldn't get out of it as easy as all that. Either she had to get married so I couldn't marry her, or I had to get married so she couldn't marry me, or we'd just have to wait till I'm twenty-six. I said Okay, we'd just have to wait unless she wanted to get married. He wrote back and said that was unlikely."

"What's she like?" I asked.

"Don't know. Not so hot, I guess, from that 'unlikely.' And I know her cousin Lawrence, and that's plenty. But if she was the season's glamour deb and it was six hundred plantations instead of six, I'm still not interested. All the same, when I ran into your Aunt Selina, I thought I'd show up just for the hell of it. I'd like to see my lost patrimony—so to speak—so I can say to my six grandchildren, 'Grandchildren, if your grandpa hadn't been a rugged individualist you'd each have had a nice big plantation down South and probably a grandma with cross-eyes and a wooden leg.' "

"What if she hadn't either?" I said.

"I'm still a rugged individualist." He grinned. "Maybe laissez-faire won't work in economics. It's still a good thing for holy matrimony. When I marry I'm going to pick the gal out all by myself. I don't care whether she's got a plantation or a job in the bargain basement. But here comes Aunt Selina. I'd better get going before she calls a cop. So long—I'll be seeing you under the magnolias."

He put one long leg over the door.and pulled the other after him with a grin, and was gone in a popping evil-smelling roar. Cornelia Cartwright stopped dead in the middle of the street and raised her hand, looking excitedly around for a non-existent policeman. Then she came hurrying over to the service station.

"Louise!" she cried. "That was that man!"

I nodded. "Yes, I was talking to him. He's very nice. He's going to Natchez."

"What for?" she demanded.

"His Aunt Selina's president of a garden club, and he's looking up a girl," I said. "He's supposed to marry her to get some property somebody left him. He's never seen her, and he wants to have a look at her."

"That's a likely story," Cornelia snapped. "I'm surprised at you for swallowing it. You ought to have more sense than to talk to people you don't know."

She got in the car and looked into the ash receiver, rather disappointed, I thought, to find her watch still there. I glanced around, waiting for Miss Letty. She was standing there, her mouth open a little, staring down the road at the disappearing trail of smoke from the old car's exhaust. She turned back to me.

"Did he say what the girl's name was?" she asked unsteadily.

"No," I said. "Just that he's supposed to marry her before he's twenty-six. But it's all right, because he's not going to. He has a quaintly naïve idea he wants to marry for love."

"That's very cynical of you, Louise," Cornelia said sharply. "Get in, Letty. We've wasted enough time as it is. Quit tinkering, Lusby."

Miss Letty got in.

"Did you say he was nice, Louise?" she asked. Something had happened to her voice. It was strained and almost inaudible.

"Very, I thought."

"Did he say what his aunt's name was?" Cornelia demanded abruptly.

"Just Aunt Selina," I said.

"Selina," she repeated thoughtfully. "There's Selina Maxwell in Philadelphia, but she's in South America. The Maxwells are *very* nice people. I'm sure he's no connection of theirs. Now look—there are some more of those absurd red and yellow ribbons. Whatever do you think they're for?"

She pointed out at half a dozen little strips of cotton cloth tied to a barbed-wire fence along a newly ploughed field.

"I asked a man back the road," I said. "They're to show it's been prospected for oil. They've found a lot of it in Louisiana. I think different companies have different colored ribbons, or something."

"But you say he isn't going to marry her?" Miss Letty interrupted, apparently unaware that the subject had been changed.

"The young man?" I asked. "No. I just said that's what he said."

"The whole thing is perfectly ridiculous on the face of it," Cornelia announced, but whether about the young man or the oil I'm not sure. "You'll have to go faster than this, Lusby. I don't care to be on these roads after dark."

She settled back in the corner, her mouth a hard, tight line. Miss Letty lapsed into silence, her gloved hands folded nervously in her lap. The softly rolling countryside in the first breathless glory of spring swept by us. As we came closer and closer to Natchez, Miss Letty's clasped hands twitched more nervously and Cornelia's mouth got tighter and tighter. I didn't realize what was disturbing her, and very acutely, until we stopped at a service station by a road sign that said *Natchez 14 Miles* to ask if we were still on the right road. Miss Letty had gone in to fix her hair. Cornelia leaned over to me.

"You know, Louise," she said, "I think we made a very serious mistake saying we'd go to Letty's old home. We should have realized if her house wasn't in the Garden Tour it wouldn't be a suitable place for us to stay." She frowned. "Maybe we can just leave her there and go to the hotel. But do be careful what you say—here she comes. Letty, Louise thinks we'd better not bother your sister and your brother—you know what having strangers descend on you is like."

Miss Letty didn't say anything at first. She just looked unhappy. Then she said, "They've probably fixed a room for you. Of course it's very old and run down."

"Of course, we expected that," Cornelia said. "All these old plantation places are."

At that moment we were passing a magnificent gleaming white portico set back in a beautifully kept park. I realized abruptly that Cornelia was comparing it with the shabby down-at-the-heel old places we'd gone by along the road, and I realized that it was her own social position she was thinking of now. I felt sorry for Miss Letty. God knows she hadn't wanted us to stay with her family.

"I think they've fixed the house up a little since I've been away," she said apologetically. "And it isn't a plantation. It's in town."

We were coming into the outskirts of Natchez. It wasn't any more depressing than the outskirts of every other town. Negro hovels with children and chickens and mangy rabbit hounds sprawling over the porches along narrow dirty streets are universal enough, heaven knows. Cornelia, however, was getting unhappier by the moment.

"We turn up Albemarle Street," Miss Letty said. "It's the house at the end of the road. Most of these have been built since I was here."

Cornelia looked at the unpretentious frame houses along the street and closed her eyes.

Lusby turned his head. "You mean this here place, miss?"

Letty nodded. "You'll have to open the gate."

Cornelia opened her eyes. In front of us were two high iron gates. One of them, under the scrolled *D*, was a white wood sign with CLOSED painted on it in black block letters. Under that was *Private Property. Not Open To The Public*. Through the gates a smooth winding road stretched through billowing masses of flaming azaleas. At the end of it, beyond the live oaks and magnolias scantily bearded with gray moss, stood one of the most imposing mansions I have ever seen.

Chapter Three

Frigid Welcome

THE HOUSE WAS RED BRICK, though it looked more mauve than red in the slanting smoky shafts of the late afternoon sun through the trees. Double galleries extended around the three sides I could see, deep and cool and shadowy from the climbing roses and eglantine twining up the high trellises between the columns. Through the long windows with their snowy arabesques of old-fashioned lace curtains, yellow points of candlelight flickered like the first fireflies at twilight. In front of the portico, looking more as if it belonged there than the smart maroon sports coupé ahead of it in the driveway, was a gleaming Victorian brougham, with a colored coachman in a blue and yellow braided uniform and top hat with a yellow band, nodding sleepily over the loosely reined pair of bored chestnut ploughhorses lazily switching each other with their tails.

Cornelia's jaw dropped. She blinked her eyes as if she thought she were still asleep.

"Why, *Letty!*" she gasped.

I looked at Miss Letty. Her hands were still folded tightly in her lap, and she kept moistening her lips with the tip of her tongue. She looked as if she were being dragged step by step closer to the guillotine. There was something else unfamiliar about her too—and all of a sudden I realized it was the locket—it was gone.

"Miss Letty!" I exclaimed.

She put out her hand quickly and gave me a look of such desperate appeal that I shut up abruptly. She moistened her lips again, smoothed her gloves and took a deep quivering breath.

"I don't wonder you're excited, Letty!" Cornelia said.

"Just think of coming home to this, after that wretched room of yours at Miss Wilson's!"

"But don't say anything about it, please—my room, I mean," Miss Letty said quickly. "It's really very comfortable."

Lusby drew up behind the carriage and put on the brakes. The coachman woke up with a start, dropped the reins and clambered down to the drive. He came tottering over to us, his hat clasped to his stomach.

"Miss Baby—is that you, Miss Baby?"

His kinky white hair was white as frost, his voice shaky with emotion.

He looked at Cornelia, getting out of her limousine like a drum major in full regimentals, looked quickly into the car and broke into a toothless grin.

"It's me, Isaac," Miss Letty said. She got out and grasped his outstretched hand.

"It's good to see you, Miss Baby," the old darky said. "Ah wouldn' ever 'a recognized you. You jus' go right along in the house. Ah'll see to everything. You come to stay, ain't you, Miss Baby?"

"Just for a few days, Isaac," Miss Letty said.

Whether I was as much affected by the unexpected externals of Miss Letty's early surroundings, and as snobbishly, as Cornelia was, I don't know—but it seemed to me that Miss Letty had suddenly taken on a new dignity. If I hadn't been right on her heels as we went up the three marble steps to the gallery, I wouldn't have realized that her steps faltered at all, or that she was steeling herself with a very real effort to face whatever it was behind the wide green door. I know she hesitated whether to open it or lift the silver hand that formed the knocker. Fortunately, it seemed to me, Cornelia didn't see that. She was standing there, looking back down the broad, beautifully kept gardens to the gate, with a sort of proprietary stance that proclaimed her the mistress of any situation, however surprising. Just then Isaac came up the steps and opened the door for us.

"Mr. Ed!" he called. "Miss Baby's come!"

I didn't see Mr. Ed coming, not right away. I was standing literally goggle-eyed in the hallway, staring around me. All my life I'd heard about Victorian grandeur, but I'd never seen it before. Then suddenly, between two ornately fruited and flowered alabaster urns at least five feet high set on elaborately carved rosewood pedestals, flanking the mahogany doors at the end of the wide reception hall, Mr. Ed appeared. He was Miss Letty made of tensile steel, and if he didn't step out of my grandmother's velvet-covered album that used to lie under the family Bible on the marble-topped table in the front parlor, he could have very easily. And he could have stepped back before he opened his lips for all of me. He wore tight-fitting buff trousers belling out a little at the cuffs, a black coat with velvet lapels, and a white ruffled shirt with some kind of a black stock under the narrow white wings of his collar. His hair was gray and his eyes, under black beetling brows, were like Miss Letty's, large and dark, except that his would have done very well for Medusa and hers were gentle and appealing. His upper lip was longer than hers, and if he'd ever smiled it was so briefly that there was no memory of it left in the sharp hard lines that slanted down from his thin nostrils almost to his lower jaw. I could see perfectly why poor Miss Letty had left Natchez, and why she had so desperately resisted having to come back.

He came forward and bowed. He didn't extend his hand to Miss Letty, or make any move to kiss her.

"I trust you had a pleasant journey, Laetitia," he said. "And these ladies?"

"This is Mrs. Cartwright," Miss Letty said quickly. "My brother, Judge Drayton. And Mrs. Gould."

Judge Drayton shook hands with Cornelia. I could see them measuring each other's arsenal for an instant, and

for once Cornelia was comparatively silent. He turned to
me.

"Mrs. Gould—it's a pleasure, I'm sure." He bowed. His
voice was about as warm as his hand.

"And this is my son."

He indicated a younger but no more modern edition
of himself who had appeared inexplicably—unless it was
from a canvas on the wall—out of the red and gold drawing-room at the right. He was dressed like his father except
that his coat was plum-colored and his trousers a kind of
puce. He had a long clay pipe in his hand. He was quite as
cold as Judge Drayton, but there was a sort of down-his-
nose air about him that made me feel like an East End ref-
ugee billeted on the unwilling upper classes.

"This is Mrs. Wainwright and Mrs. Gould—"

"Cartwright," said Cornelia.

"—and your Aunt Laetitia, whom you may remember,"
said the Judge. "My son, Lawrence Drayton. The maid
will show you to your rooms. My sister is dressing. She will
meet you later. We dine at two o'clock. I trust you will enjoy your stay in Natchez. It is the only place left where you
will find the gracious hospitality of the Old South uninflu-
enced by the commercialism of the modern world."

What I should have done, of course, was turn around
and go back to the car. But I didn't; I was too stunned. I
followed Cornelia and the colored maid with Lusby and
old Isaac bringing our bags through the alabaster urns
into a wide foyer with doors opening onto the back gallery and an elegant staircase curving up one side. Miss
Letty, also stunned after her brief blossoming at the portico, came beside me.

"If you'll just wait a moment, miss," the maid said to
me, "I'll take this lady to her room first. You're upstairs,
Miss Laetitia."

"It's really charming, Letty," Cornelia said. "Perfectly
charming!"

She marched off, and Miss Letty just stood there, inarticulately wretched, staring at the floor, her lips trembling.

"Oh, don't!" I whispered. "Please don't!"

She turned to me quickly, and stood staring, her eyes fixed past me on something at the end of the hall, the color draining slowly out of her cheeks. She swayed a little, and put out her hand to the stair rail to steady herself. She looked as if she were seeing a ghost, and for a moment, when I turned around, I certainly thought I was.

In the vaguely smoky shaft of sunlight slanting across the gallery through the open door was a figure as light and intangible as thistledown. It was a girl, her hair the color of molten gold, a red rose caught in the bright coronet of upswept curls, her white lace dress cut low over the shoulders, draped in festoons and caught with scarlet velvet bows over the broad hoops that filled the doorway. She came forward, her white satin ballet slippers with red velvet ribbons crisscrossed around her slender ankles noiseless on the polished floor. She came toward us quickly, her hoops swaying gracefully with the movement of her body. There was no doubt that she was very real and very live. Her bare suntanned shoulders were warm and smooth as satin, her eyes were dark like Mr. Ed's but soft like Miss Letty's, and set wide apart under long dark lashes and delicately arched brows, in a face that was breathtakingly lovely.

Miss Letty took a faltering half-step toward her.

"Anne?" she whispered.

"Aunt Letty?"

The girl's eyes lighted, her red lips broke into a radiant smile. She held out her arms.

"How wonderful! You've come at last—I knew you would!"

Miss Letty stumbled forward, and the girl caught her in her arms and held her tight. Her eyes were suddenly dark with anger.

"They were horrible to you, weren't they?" she whispered passionately. "You poor darling! How dared they be!"

She looked down the stairs, her eyes blazing.

"They won't any more. You have as much right here as anybody. Don't cry—please don't! I'll take care of you."

Miss Letty raised her head. The girl kissed her, her own eyes bright with tears. I looked around. The maid was coming from Cornelia's room.

"Which is my aunt's room, Mamie?" Anne Drayton asked. "She's tired, and wants to lie down."

"She's upstairs, Miss Anne. I'll take her bag—"

Anne's eyes darkened again. The warm flush deepened in her cheeks.

"Take my aunt's bag to my room," she said quietly.

"But Miss Kate said—"

"Take her bag to my room."

As the maid went off, Anne turned and held her hand out to me. "I'm Anne Drayton," she said, with a smile that didn't entirely conceal the anger she still felt.

"Oh, I'm sorry," Miss Letty whispered. "This is Louise—"

The girl smiled again, really this time.

"Hello, Louise. I'm glad you've come. I haven't seen Aunt Letty since I was a little girl. You're over there in the rose room next to us. If you want anything just ring and Mamie will come—and if she doesn't just ring until she does."

I followed Mamie and Lusby into the rose room, waited a moment until they'd gone, and stepped through the open window onto the balcony. I was angry, too. I was angry at Cornelia Cartwright for getting us into this, and angrier at Mr. Ed—Judge Drayton, I suppose I should call him—for being so cruel to poor Miss Letty—and also at myself for not having had spunk enough to leave at the front door. And I wasn't staying a night under that roof if I had to sleep on somebody's doorstep.

A cool breeze fragrant with roses and honeysuckle touched my burning cheeks. I looked out over the grounds. The lawns stretched like smooth velvet to the massed dogwood, redbud, and pink and white azaleas along the brick wall, to where the garden ended and sloped suddenly off into a tangle of vines interwoven among the great white spears of Spanish dagger, and past that into a deep gully that they call a bayou down here. Through the leafy screen of trees and flowers I could see the two chimneys and slanting roof of another house across the bayou. A soft shadowy haze hung over everything, making it fragile and lovely and a kind of fairyland, remote and unreal. It seemed incredible that just inside was something that was very real indeed, and not very lovely—a little terrifying, really.

There must, of course, be something behind it, I thought, to have made it that way. Miss Letty was obviously some kind of an outcast—and they could treat her as one, and she accepted it as if in some strange way it was her due. Her sister hadn't even come down to greet her after she'd been away for years. She was going to put her up in what would be a kind of attic, I supposed from the anger that suddenly blazed in Anne Drayton's eyes. Anne, I supposed, was Judge Drayton's daughter. All in all, it seemed like a very odd family to me, what with Miss Letty's poverty compared with the wealth of the family home.

I stood there sort of getting myself together to tell Cornelia I wasn't staying, trying to figure it out without very much to go on, I'm afraid, when I heard Miss Letty's voice. She must have moved closer to the window, because I hadn't been conscious of hearing her before.

"But he's here now," she was saying. "Louise was talking to him today. He's coming to see you."

Anne Drayton laughed.

"He's certainly taken his time about it. Anyway, he

wrote that he didn't want to marry me. And I certainly don't want to marry him. I wouldn't have married him for anything in the world. If he wants the plantations he's welcome to them."

"But you might like him."

"*Like* Steve Heywood!" she exclaimed. "Aunt Letty—you don't *know* him!"

"You don't either, do you, Anne?"

"No, but Lawrence does. He's told me about him. He's simply insufferable. Anyway, it's too late. It hasn't been announced, so it's still a secret, but I'm going to be married in July."

For a moment there was a dead silence. I shouldn't have been listening, of course, but I don't think I could have torn myself away if I'd tried—which it didn't, I'm afraid, occur to me to do.

"Don't look so stunned, darling," Anne went on then. "It's not so bad as all that. After all, I have to marry sometime."

"Who—who is it?" I heard Miss Letty ask.

"You'll be surprised. It's Lawrence."

I heard Miss Letty repeat the name blankly, and I thought, *Lawrence—that's that unpleasant young man in pantaloons with a clay pipe that we met downstairs.*

"It does sound funny, doesn't it?"

Anne's voice was a little wistful, it seemed to me.

"I know he's my cousin, but you see, Uncle Ed has taken care of me just as if I were his daughter. It must have cost him a lot, and he's always been very generous. He wants me to, and so does Aunt Kate."

She laughed. "And so does Lawrence, since he came home from law school at Christmas. And I'm very fond of him, really. He's always been nice to me, and he's changed a lot. Don't look so distressed, Aunt Letty. I'll be very happy—or just as happy as most people, anyway."

I thought, *Oh, dear,* and started back to my room. But

before I got to the window I heard a door open and Anne's voice.

"Here's Aunt Letty, Aunt Kate! Tell her you're glad to see her!"

A cool voice spoke.

"I'm very glad to see her," Miss Kate Drayton was saying. "And now I want to see her alone. Go in my room, Anne, and help Mamie with my dress."

I heard the door open and close again, and then a long silence. It was broken by Miss Kate's voice, as cold and hostile as her brother's and with the same steely quality.

"If you've come to make trouble, Laetitia, I shall ask you and your friends to leave at once. If you had any pride or decency you'd not show your face in this house. I know why you've come. Perhaps I can even understand it. Now you've seen for yourself how little we need you, you must go away. We won't allow you to come here and upset everything. And I won't allow you to be here with Anne. Anne is ours. She has nothing to do with you. Your room is upstairs. We will treat your friends as honored guests, but we expect you to leave as soon as you possibly can. And I say again, we refuse to allow you to make trouble in this house. Is that clear, Laetitia?"

I could almost see Miss Letty shrinking before that lashing icy attack.

"Can't you speak?" her sister demanded.

"I didn't come back to make trouble," Miss Letty said unhappily. "I'm very grateful to you. But I have a right to come here if I want to. It's as much mine as it is yours and Ed's. And there's one thing I won't allow."

Miss Kate's voice was full of icy scorn. "You? *Allow?*"

"Yes. That's what I said. And I mean it. Anne's not going to marry Lawrence: You can't do that. That's what I won't allow."

There was a long silence. Then Miss Kate said, "Brother and I will discuss that matter with you later, Laetitia."

I went back into my room with a kind of sick and at the same time angry feeling in the pit of my stomach. What could Miss Letty have done, I wondered, that could have turned her brother and sister against her so bitterly? They must have some quality of kindness in them to make Anne speak of them with such obvious gratitude. She was apparently marrying the frozen-faced young man with the puce pantaloons and the churchwarden pipe because they wanted her to, but not because they were compelling her to. She was acting of her own free will, which coincided with their wishes. But that if it hadn't, and she had wanted to marry someone else? I wondered. What—for instance—if she'd met Steve Heywood, and decided she'd marry him?

I found myself smiling in spite of everything. Each of them had a surprise coming—and on the whole, the fact that he didn't apparently like Lawrence and Lawrence thought he was insufferable made it rather more interesting. But I'd forgot for the moment I wasn't going to be there to see them.

I started to the door to find Cornelia to tell her I was leaving, and stopped when she opened it herself and stepped in.

"My dear, isn't this utterly divine?" she exclaimed. "We must take some pictures and send them home immediately. I could shake Letty for not telling me."

"I think it's foul," I said. "I wonder if Lusby could take me downtown?"

"What for!" Cornelia cried. "Why, Louise—whatever is the matter?"

"I just don't like the way they treat Miss Letty, in the first place," I said. "And in the second they don't want us here, and I don't blame them, exactly. We stuffed ourselves down their throats. I don't wonder they gagged. Anyway, they dined at two and it's getting on to seven and I'm hungry."

"I think when you're in Rome you're expected to do as

Rome does, Louise," Cornelia said stiffly.

"Even Nero didn't say you couldn't leave Rome," I retorted.

"You don't seem to realize it's a great privilege to be allowed to stay here, Louise."

"I'm sure it is. I just happen to feel unworthy of it."

"Well, if it's on Letty's account you're being very silly," Cornelia said. "There's obviously some very good reason why she's never been back here, and has been as mum as the grave all these years. I'd like *very much* to know what it is."

"I wouldn't," I said. "But whatever it is, I'm on Miss Letty's side. And I'm not asking you to leave. You can stay. I'm going."

"Then you'll have to arrange for your own transportation. Lusby has gone downtown to get his supper."

She wheeled and went out, shutting the door sharply behind her. In less than half a minute, it seemed to me, she was back.

"Louise! That man! He's still following us—he's coming up the drive! And my watch—I left it in the car!"

"I hope Lusby locked it," I said. I picked up my gloves and handbag.

"Louise, what are you doing?" she demanded.

"I'm going to ask the young man—Steve Heywood's his name—to take me downtown. I'll let you know where I am."

I went out and down the stairs.

Judge Drayton and his son Lawrence were just starting up. Old Isaac in his other capacity of butler appeared in the door as they stood aside for me to come down.

"Mr. Ed, that there man's done come," Isaac said.

Judge Drayton turned. "What man, Isaac?"

The old darky held out a salver with a visiting-card on it.

"That there man yo' said Ah wasn' on no account to let come in this here house. The one that's done come after

Miss Anne. Mr. Steven Heywood is his name."

Judge Drayton glanced quickly at his son. It seemed to me there was a definite quality of anxiety, if not actual alarm, in both their faces. He took the card, looked at it, and looked at his son again.

"News leaks out fast," Lawrence Drayton said. His smile was sardonic and not amused. "Who do you suppose told him?"

His father shook his head briefly. It wasn't in answer to his question, however—it was a warning for him to hold his tongue. Lawrence glanced up at me quickly.

Judge Drayton handed the salver back to Isaac. "Where is he?" he asked.

"He's restin' hisself on th' front gallery, Mr. Ed."

"I'll talk to him. You stay here, Lawrence."

He went across the parquet floor with sharp decisive steps and disappeared into the outer hall. I came on down the stairs.

"It's just a fellow that's been making himself a blasted nuisance about my cousin Anne," Lawrence said. He gave the impression of feeling that some explanation of this breach of Southern hospitality was necessary, or at least desirable.

"Really?" I said.

He nodded absently. He was listening to what was going on at the front door. He didn't have to exert himself particularly. It was perfectly audible.

"Good evening, sir. I'm Steven Heywood."

The young man's voice was warm and friendly in spite of his having been left to rest himself on the gallery.

"I was passing through Natchez, and thought I would like to have the pleasure of calling on Miss Drayton while I'm in town."

"I'm sorry, Mr. Heywood," Judge Drayton said. "Miss Drayton is indisposed. I will tell her you called."

His tone was such that the quiet closing of the door

would have been the perfect punctuation mark.

"I'm not leaving until after lunch tomorrow," Steve Heywood said equably. "Perhaps I can call again in the morning."

"I'm sorry, Mr. Heywood. My niece will be unable to receive you tomorrow or at any future time," Judge Drayton replied calmly. "I assure you it is her own decision. I shall ask you not to persist in forcing yourself upon her, sir."

"That's telling him," Lawrence whispered, with obvious satisfaction.

There was a short silence from the outer hall. Then Steve Heywood said, "I see. Then will you tell Miss Drayton I have no intention of forcing myself upon her. And will you kindly present my compliments to her uncle and tell him I said the hell with him? Good night, sir."

"I guess that's telling him too," I couldn't help but say.

The door closed abruptly. Lawrence Drayton looked at me as if I couldn't possibly have said what he thought I'd said. His father came back into the room. If it was possible for his face to have a steelier cast it had one.

"That settles that young scoundrel," he said softly. A thin smile played on his lips. "I don't expect we'll have any more trouble with him."

He turned to me. "Mr. Heywood is a young upstart who is presuming on an unfortunately worded legal document to make my niece's acquaintance, Mrs. Gould," he said casually. "You're coming to the candlelight ball with us, aren't you? I think you'll enjoy a very unusual sight in these days. Ah—here comes my niece. As my guest, Mrs. Gould, I shall ask you to say nothing to her about the person who called. I don't want to disturb her."

I looked up the stairway. Anne Drayton, too radiantly and vividly alive for the hampering hoops of a nostalgic dream world that died in the blood and tears of three-quarters of a century ago, was coming gaily down.

"Who was that at the door, Uncle Ed?" she asked expectantly.

"A Yankee tourist who can't read signs," Judge Drayton said calmly. "We'll have to station Isaac down at the gate until the Pilgrimage is over, I'm afraid."

Anne laughed. "I just thought it might be that awful Heywood man. Aunt Letty said he was in town at last."

Her uncle looked at her sharply.

"That's something you don't have to worry your head about, my dear."

Her face clouded for an instant.

"I'm not, Uncle Ed. I just thought it might be a good chance for you to see him and make some kind of fair settlement about the estate."

"You can leave all that to me, Anne," the Judge said.

"Oh, I know."

She flashed back to her carefree self again. "You're coming to the ball with us, aren't you, Louise? You don't have to dress. Most of the visitors don't."

I looked from Judge Drayton to his son. I had a curious sense of some kind of a conspiracy—if that isn't too strong a word—between them in relation to Anne that was more than just a simple desire to keep her for themselves. In that conspiracy, Anne was the stake, in some way, and completely and naïvely unaware of it. And it was not because Lawrence Drayton was in love with her. If he was in any degree, there weren't any signs of it that I could see. I made up my mind abruptly.

"I'd love to," I said. "And I'll change. I wonder if I can use the phone before we go?"

"It's in the library." She indicated the room to the left of the hallway.

I said, "Thanks," and hurried back up the stairs. I'd give Steve Heywood ten minutes to get back to the hotel, I thought. If he turned up at the candlelight ball that I knew was given for visiting Pilgrims, I could safely leave the rest to Fate.

I was just scrambling into a long dress when there was a tap at my door.

"Come in," I said.

It was Miss Letty. Her face was pale and tense.

"Louise," she said quickly. "Cornelia tells me you're going—away."

"I'm afraid we're a terrible nuisance to your family," I said.

She came to me quickly and took my hand.

"Please—don't go. I know it's terrible—but please, for my sake, don't go! I need you. Please stick it out!"

I looked at my watch. My ten minutes were almost up.

"All right," I said. "What hotel would anybody be most likely to stay at here?"

She gave me a name. Then she looked at me sharply. "It's not—"

I nodded. A light brightened her harassed eyes. She glanced back at the door. "Don't let them find out," she whispered, and went out.

I wiped the extra lipstick off my mouth and went out into the empty hall and down the stairs. No one was in sight. I hurried into the library, glanced at the list of numbers on the pad beside the phone and got the operator.

"Is Mr. Steven Heywood registered with you?" I asked when the room clerk answered.

"He's just checked out," he answered. "He left about three minutes ago. Wait a minute—I'll see if I can catch him."

I heard him call a boy, and waited. In a moment he said, "I'm sorry. His car's gone."

"Thank you," I said. I put down the phone and glanced up. Judge Drayton was standing in the doorway.

Chapter Four

BALL INTO BRAWL

THE CANDLELIGHT BALL was well under way when we arrived—Cornelia, Miss Letty, and I, with Miss Kate Drayton accompanying us to show Lusby the way. For a moment as we came up to the steps from the drive, the illusion of having set the clock back to another far-off, simpler, and more romantic day was quite complete. The dancing yellow tips of hundreds of candles shone softly through the vine-secluded windows and through the wide-open door like rows of orderly golden bees, and picked out the lacy wrought-iron pilasters and cornice of the double gallery. The women with their swaying hoops, flowers in their hair, their bare shoulders luminously soft in the shadowy light, were lovely. The whole atmosphere was one of lilting gaiety, as if every one had caught, to believe in for a moment, the brief illusory reality of this escape from the present world.

For an instant I was caught in it too, and then I became conscious of the cars crowded behind us in the drive, trying to find a parking-space, and of the other visitors like Miss Letty and myself in modern dress. It was we who gave it the air of make-believe, not the make-believe itself. I turned to say something about it to Cornelia. But I'd underestimated her capacity for protective coloration. She'd come in costume, and she'd spotted somebody from the gallery steps, and she was not only already through the receiving line but in it, welcoming the guests, native and alien, as graciously as if her grandfather had fought with the Gray at Vicksburg instead of hiring an impoverished neighbor to represent him there with the Blue. I'm sure Cornelia will receive next to St. Peter at the Pearly Gates.

I shook hands with her. She bent forward a little.

"Louise," she whispered. "That man. He's still follow-ing us. Now don't say he isn't because he is. I saw him sneaking up on the porch, looking in the window."

"It must be somebody else," I said. "He's gone. He's left Natchez."

"Then it's somebody else that looks just like him."

"He's got cousins down here," I said reassuringly. "It's probably a cousin. Did you find your watch?"

"I forgot to look. You'd better call Lusby and have him lock the car."

I went on, not particularly interested, Cornelia's ideas having ways of becoming fixations—like the time she de-cided her postman looked like one of the Dillinger mob and raised Cain until he was transferred to another part of town.

I glanced around the room. Lawrence Drayton was sur-rounded at the punchbowl by what I think they call a bevy of girls. Anne was at the other side of the room with Miss Letty surrounded by women in varying degrees of ante-bellum costume who seemed delighted to see her again. Miss Letty looked happier than I'd ever seen her. Her brother and sister were standing behind them in the door-way, tight-lipped and stiff and, I thought, a little annoyed.

I wandered through the candle-lit rooms, looking at the house. It wasn't magnificent like the Drayton house, but it had a lived-in air and a kind of shadowy glamour in the dancing minuet of the tiny lights that was very pleasant. I came out onto the back gallery, and stopped abruptly. Sit-ting on a saddle on a rack just outside the door was a young man in dinner jacket. He was smoking a cigarette, and his face in the pale eerie light was about as grim as anything I've seen. I stared at him, and he stared back at me. Sud-denly he broke into a broad grin.

"Hi," he said. He held out a big paw.

"I thought you'd gone!" I gasped.

"Sssh," he said. "I did go. I got ten miles out, and decided I'd come back."

"What for?"

He got up. "What about a turn in the garden, ma'am?"

"My name's Gould, Louise Gould," I said. "And if there's a vegetable garden, I'd like a raw potato. I'm starved. I'd rather have a hamburger. I don't dare drink any punch until I've had something."

"I want you to do me a favor, and then we'll go get one," Steve Heywood said.

We went down the steps and out into a moonlit garden that was overgrown and full of a tangled charm that the grounds of Antigua—which was the name of the Drayton place—were far too well kept to have.

"I want you to find out which is Anne Drayton, and show her to me," he went on.

"I already know. That's where we're staying."

"You are!" he exclaimed. "Then you've met the old museum piece in the monkey suit."

"That's Judge Drayton," I said. "He's the fine flower of traditional hospitality."

"Or something."

"And I've seen the girl."

"I'm not interested," he said.

"I thought you wanted me to show her to you."

"I do. But that's not why I came back."

"Then why did you?" I demanded.

"Just to get even with the whole pack of 'em." He looked at me with a kind of grim cheerfulness that was rather disconcerting. "I don't want the plantations, and I certainly don't want to marry any cross-eyed Southern bud."

"How did you know she was cross-eyed?"

"I told you I knew a cousin of hers who's at law school in New Haven. Lawrence Drayton. He told me a lot about her."

I said, "Oh."

"Anyway, that was just last fall, and I didn't have any intention of ever looking her up even then, so that's not the point. The point is, nobody shuts the door in *my* face and gets away with it. I've got two weeks before I have to show up to risk my neck—cheerfully as a matter of fact—to keep these people's world all wrapped up in pink cotton. And I'm going to enjoy myself making it damned uncomfortable for the whole crew of 'em. I don't remember the will exactly, but boy, oh, boy, is Miss Anne going to wish she hadn't been indisposed! And is Uncle going to wish he hadn't shut the door in little Stevie's face!"

I looked at him, sitting there grinning like an ape and apparently enjoying himself enormously. It wasn't all amusement. There was a pretty determined serious undertone that curiously enough was entirely without bitterness. He was sore, but he wasn't hurt.

"I never did like Lawrence, anyway," he said.

"But what if it's not Anne's fault?" I asked. "She didn't even know you were there this evening. And she can't help it if she's cross-eyed."

"Well, she shouldn't have let herself be born in that family then," Steve Heywood said cheerfully.

I glanced up. Coming along the path, the moonlight silvering her shining hair, was the girl we were talking about, ethereally lovely as a dream.

"Gosh!" Steve said—or whistled, rather.

Anne Drayton and an older man, obviously a stranger she was showing the garden, turned off along another path. For an instant I started to call her, and then I decided it wouldn't hurt Steve to wait a little longer. In fact I thought it might be rather good for him.

"You don't happen to know *her*, do you?" he said, still following her with an admiring and slightly awe-struck gaze.

"Why don't we go inside?" I said. I got up. "Your old friend Lawrence is in there, holding down the punchbowl.

If he introduces you to his Aunt Kate, they'll have to let you in Antigua. Then they'll have to introduce you to Anne too. If they don't, I will. She's going to marry Lawrence, by the way, if that happens to interest you. It's a secret I'm not supposed to know, so don't tell anybody."

He'd started to follow me up the path,.but he stopped abruptly at that.

"The hell she is," he said blankly. Then he grinned. "This gets better and better. I'm sure glad I happened in. I wouldn't have missed this—not for nothing."

I wouldn't either, I thought. I really thought it then. Later I wasn't sure I wouldn't have given almost anything to have missed it.

I went inside first. I didn't want Judge Drayton to see me with him, not being quite certain whether he'd heard whom I'd been phoning to. He'd come to get a cigar, he'd said, and hoped I'd excuse his intrusion; but it had seemed to me there was some added expression in the hard angle of lines at the end of his lips.

I slipped unobtrusively into the crowded dining-room. Lawrence Drayton was leaning against the mahogany sideboard, the center of a group of young people. His father was across the room, and neither Miss Kate nor Miss Letty was in sight. Judge Drayton was talking, or listening rather, to the two women Cornelia had greeted with surprised enthusiasm as we came in. Either of them might have been Steve's Aunt Selina, or Cornelia herself for that matter. They were well-fed and well-corseted ladies, with smartly coiffed white hair, and rouge a little too pink and powder a little too white. One had a lorgnette and the other rimless pince-nez, and they were both talking at once—one about what her club had done to the highways in California, and the other about the rhododendrons her club had planted around their city dump in Minnesota. Judge Drayton was listening, but his heart wasn't in it. Every time he nodded his head he cast a sharp sidelong glance at his son, a frown gathering between his heavy brows.

Lawrence had apparently felt the need of fortification, and was rather noisier than the ritualistic dignity of the occasion seemed to warrant.

"We were too smart to let the damyankees burn down *our* houses," he was saying to a pretty girl in tweeds, obviously a Pilgrim. "We were the appeasers of that day. We invited the officers in and—"

He stopped abruptly. His face went the color of a dismayed oyster. His eyes blinked and his mouth sagged open just enough to make everybody around him turn to see what manner of ghost had risen out of the old walls to silence such blasphemy as he'd been speaking. And Steve Heywood was wonderful. He was making his way between the ladies' hoops, a good head and shoulders above nearly everybody in the room, with a cheerful "Well, fancy meeting you here of all places, old fellow!" air that couldn't have been more convincing if he'd meant it.

"Larry, my boy!" he said, grinning. He thrust out his hand.

Lawrence's jaw snapped shut. A bright flush colored his cheekbones.

"Hello," he said stiffly. "What are you doing around here?"

I looked quickly at Judge Drayton. I've never been sure what an obelisk is, but if it's what I think it is, that's what he looked like at the moment. Inside, I mean. Outwardly there wasn't the least change. He went on listening courteously to how the Pilgrim from California had, singlehanded, picketed a eucalyptus tree in front of a chain store until the Governor himself had stepped in and refused to allow it to be cut down. He managed to detach himself then and moved away, and I looked back at Steve and Lawrence.

"Oh, I was just in town," I'd heard Steve say. "I thought I'd drop in to see the show so I could make time with Aunt

Selina. I've got a little business down here. A cousin of my father's left me some run-down plantations. I figured I'd better have a look at them. Old Minot Heywood. I guess maybe you knew him, didn't you?"

The flush on Lawrence Drayton's cheekbones darkened.

"I knew him," he said unpleasantly. "I didn't know he left them to you. I thought he left them to my cousin Anne."

"By golly, I forgot!" Steve exclaimed. "She *is* your cousin, isn't she? That's a blow. I hoped she'd be a nice gal. I'm supposed to marry her."

I thought for an instant—to put it inelegantly—that Lawrence was going to bust. He controlled himself with what is called a superhuman effort.

"If that's what you're down here for, you can go back where you came from," he said angrily. "My cousin has no intention of marrying you, or anybody like you."

"So I've heard," Steve said. "But I'm afraid she'll have to. *If* she wants to get the plantations."

Lawrence's laugh was the kind I'd thought went out with the old villains in melodrama. "The hell she does. You'd better read the will again and brush up on your law."

"I just read it, as a matter of fact," Steve said. "It says, if I'm unwilling to conform to the terms set forth herein the property goes to the lady."

He gave Lawrence a beaming smile.

"But I'm not unwilling—see? It doesn't say what happens if she's unwilling. Which, frankly, I can't imagine."

It really wasn't fair. Lawrence was under the influence, as they used to put it, and he'd lost his temper from the start. And Steve's elaborate sanctimoniousness couldn't have been more infuriating.

"After all, you know, Larry," he went on suavely, "it's not that I want to marry your cousin. It was my father's poor dear cousin's dying wish. It's my duty, in spite of everything."

I saw Judge Drayton, halfway to the door, come to an abrupt halt. A quick gleam of satisfaction lighted his face. As I looked past him my heart gave a ghastly double jump into my mouth and back with a sickening lurch into the pit of my stomach. Anne Drayton was standing there, and there wasn't the shadow of a doubt from the look on her exquisite face that she'd heard the whole silly business. She took a quick step forward, her eyes blazing. Her uncle went to her and took her by the shoulders, shaking his head. For an instant I thought she was going to break loose, but she relaxed suddenly, turned and went out with him into the hall. Neither Steve Heywood nor Lawrence had seen her. Steve's back was to the door, and Lawrence was too furious to be conscious of anything. He was trembling with rage.

"You big redheaded baboon," he said, "you're not coming down here and getting away with that line! Where have you been all these years? What about your poor dear cousin's dying wish all that time? Now we've made a strike, you come sneaking around. You think you're going to cash in—we'll see you in hell first!"

His voice broke incoherently. Then, without the slightest warning, he threw the punch cup in his hand straight at Steve's head. There was a stifled scream from the girls near him. I thought for a moment that the candlelight ball was turning into a good old-fashioned Natchez-under-the-Hill brawl. Steve stood there. He hadn't moved except for a left hand flashing up in front of his face, so quick that I couldn't follow it. He looked down for an instant at Lawrence Drayton trying to wrench his arms loose from the grasp of a couple of friends. Then he put the punch cup calmly down on the table, turned and came across the room to me.

"Did you say you wanted a hamburger, Louise?" he asked equably.

Chapter Five

LETHAL DOSE OF ROMANCE

WE'D MADE OUR WAY through the crowded rooms almost to the door when Cornelia intercepted me.

"Louise—Miss Kate had a headache," she said. "Judge Drayton and Anne have taken her home. We should be going shortly ourselves."

Then she looked up at Steve. Her face went a mottled green. "Louise!" she gasped.

"Oh, I'm sorry," I said. "I don't think you've met, have you? Mrs. Cartwright, Mr. Heywood. Mrs. Selina Maxwell's nephew, you know."

Cornelia looked at him skeptically—as well she might. His shirt front was wet, with little bits of lemon pulp adhering to it, and his collar had definitely seen better moments. But Cornelia was a lady. She took a deep breath.

"How do you do, Mr. Maxwell?" she said.

Steve bowed.

"I think we'd better be going at once, Louise. We don't want to keep the Draytons up waiting for us. I'll just run and say good-by to Millicent and Cora and arrange for luncheon tomorrow. You didn't meet them when they visited me last year after the James River Pilgrimage, did you? It was when you were in Rochester with the Doctor. Mrs. Gould's husband is a doctor, and a charming gentleman."

She added that last to Steve, significantly, as if he were neither, and further might possibly be under some illusion that I was not only unattached but much younger than my obvious thirty-five. She also gave me a disapproving glance as if I too might not have considered my husband and my age.

"Mrs. Gould is going with me to get a sandwich," Steve said. "I'll get her home all right."

Cornelia's lips tightened. Whether it was my life or my reputation she feared for, I wouldn't know. She obviously couldn't make a scene just then, not with Millicent and Cora bearing down on us from the other end of the hall. Anyway, we got out, just as the Draytons' car started off. I saw Judge Drayton's face, the sort of pale greenish hue that faces have through the processed glass of motor windows, his eyes fixed on me, and not very pleasantly either. He must have leaned over to tell Anne, because I saw her face for an instant too, looking at me, curiously white through the window, her eyes like two great dark stars.

"There she is, Steve—quick!" I said.

"Where?"

But it was too late. She'd leaned back against the cushions again, and the long car moved down the drive.

"And she heard you, by the way, if you'd care to know it," I said when we'd got into his car and started to follow them down the narrow wooded road to the highway.

He didn't say anything for a moment. I looked at him. The debonair and amusing devil-may-care young man that he'd been up to the time Lawrence hurled the punch cup was gone. In his place was a hard-jawed and steely-eyed person I hadn't met before.

"That's okay with me," he said at last.

"You wouldn't want to appear rude, would you?" I asked sweetly.

"She must be used to it, living with Lawrence and the Judge," he returned. "As a matter of fact, I'm sorry. If I'd known she was there I wouldn't have done it. Or maybe I would. If she's like the rest of them, she's got it coming to her."

"What if you have to marry her?" I inquired. "You said publicly you were willing, you know. And just wait till you have a look at her."

We pulled up at a roadside stand. He sat there, just looking grim, until the colored boy brought us our hamburgers and coffee.

"You know," he said, "this isn't quite as funny as I thought it was. I don't mean I'm afraid they'll make me marry her. You can always leave town in a hurry. It's—"

He stopped and bit into his hamburger, and sat there chewing thoughtfully.

"You know, Louise," he said, "there's something funny about this. I never figured out why Minot Heywood made such a cockeyed will in the first place. If he wanted to leave his property outside the family, why didn't he do it and be done with it? I suppose it was just a gesture, as a matter of fact. He pulled a fast one on my father and got Dad's share of the family fortunes as well as his own. He wrote the will himself. It went like this: 'In order to repair a great wrong, so that I can sleep peacefully through eternity, I leave my entire estate, real and personal, and so on, to Steven Heywood, son of my beloved cousin Steven Heywood, if on or before his twenty-sixth birthday he married Anne Drayton, and so on.' "

"Thereby doing another great wrong, you think, I suppose," I said.

He gave me a sour grin.

"It just happens that my father did all right by himself and forgot all about it," he said. "My mother used to remember it, not very seriously—just every time she went to an antique sale. Something to make the old man come across with, like, 'Well, dearest, if you'd got the portraits and that table you should have had, I wouldn't have to buy these things.' You know how women are."

"I know," I said.

"Anyway, I sort of figured the gal might need the property and I didn't, and it was cockeyed anyway, trying to marry people off by last will and testament. Then I come down here and find she's as well heeled as I am, if not better. Even at that, I'd have been willing to pass it up. But what griped me was the idea I was horning in on something I hadn't any right to—slamming the door in my face because I was forcing my unwelcome attentions on the little lady."

"I've already told you that wasn't her fault," I said.

"All right. Leave her out if you like. But you heard Cousin Lawrence—I'd waited till they'd made a strike, and then down I barge to cash in?"

I nodded.

"That smells fishy to me. I don't know what he's talking about, but off-hand it looks to me like Larry and his old pappy know something I don't. They're trying to pull something fast and dirty."

"Well," I said, "if you don't want to marry the girl—"

"And that's more of the same," he interrupted. "Last fall Larry didn't want to marry her either. He was playing around with a cute little raven-haired number in New York every week-end. The way he described his cousin Anne would make a Hungarian count head for Sitka even if he knew she had five million in gold doubloons."

"Would he be trying to scare you off?" I asked.

He shook his head. "Maybe—but the gal in New York certainly thought he was going to marry her, not Cousin Anne. Anyway, I'm perfectly willing to stand aside for a lady, but I'm not letting Larry and the Judge make hay at Steven's expense."

"Then it's not a joke any longer."

"You're damn right it's not. Not until I see what's up. And not until I'm sure Anne Drayton's getting the money and not Cousin Lawrence. Cousin Minot must have thought it was going to be uphill work to get her a husband and wanted her to have the estate to swing it with—but I don't think he figured on her buying a dud like Lawrence. Anyway, I'm going to have a look-see. I think there's something screwy about it."

He took my coffee cup and put it on the tray at the window.

"Well, well," he said. "As I live and breathe!"

He pointed to a shiny black limousine pulling in beside an oil truck in front of us. "Aunt Selina! In duplicate!"

I looked quickly. I didn't know whether it really was his Aunt Selina or just Cornelia again. As a matter of fact it wasn't either. It was Cornelia's friends, Millicent, the lone picket of the eucalyptus tree, and Cora, of rhododendrons around the city dump. The white uniformed chauffeur got out and opened the door.

"What would you like, madam?" he asked.

"A hot dog, Bates. What will you have, Cora?"

"A hot dog," Cora said. "With mustard. And a cup of coffee."

"Coffee keeps me awake," Millicent said. "Are you sure you want coffee?"

"Coffee doesn't keep me awake," Cora returned. "That's all imagination."

"Two hot dogs and one cup of coffee, Bates," Millicent said.

The chauffeur repeated it to the wall-eyed colored boy standing by. It sounded, as he said it, rather like two orders of quail and one of champagne.

"Coffee keeps me awake," Millicent said.

"The hot dog," Steve observed, "is a great democratic leveler. What about another hamburger?"

"No, thanks," I said. "I've got to get along before they pull up the drawbridge. I'm not even sure they're going to let me in, considering the company I keep. Anyway, there's a man behind us that wants our space."

He pulled out in front of the limousine and the oil truck. The small black car that was waiting came in behind us. I saw the two ladies looking at it critically. The curiously sallow-faced man behind the wheel struck his horn sharply, and the colored boy hurried out to him.

It really wouldn't have surprised me to have found the wrought iron gates of Antigua locked and barred, but they weren't. In fact, they were standing open.

"It's beautiful, isn't it?" I said. It really was. The silvery moonlight touched trees and lawns with phosphorescent magic. The azaleas along the circling drive were like banks of rosy snow. Through the oaks and magnolias with their streamers of moss as intangible as wisps of pale smoke on the horizon, stood the great house. Its columns rose like gracious sentinels, gleaming softly in the silvered night; its frosted slate roof shone liquid as water. Under it beyond the columns the deep recesses of the galleries were a shadowy moat concealing and securing the walls inside. A faint yellow glow through the broad elliptical fanlight over the door was the only sign that Antigua was more than a lovely ghost sleeping in an enchanted garden.

"It's phony romance," Steve said, answering me.

"Rot," I said.

"That's what it is. It's escape. A retreat from functionalism. It's all rhetoric and no grammar, if you know what I mean. It's an anachronism. It's outlived its time and purpose. Now take good modern architecture. That's functional—grammar and logic. For use, not show."

"Oh, pooh," I said. "What you need is a good dose of spiritual sulphur and molasses."

As I said it I had no idea of what an almost lethal dose of it Fate, or whatever, had stirred up for him and was waiting with just around a narrow corner.

We went up the drive in front of the house. Steve stopped and pulled on his brake.

"What you need," he said, "is a little hard-boiled realism."

We got out. He started up to the door with me, his feet scrunching on the graveled roadway.

"You weren't such a realist when I met you this morning," I said. "Unless it's a new kind of realism to refuse an estate that's dropped in your lap."

"Yeah, but that's all changed now," he returned.

As we came up to the broad low steps leading to the gallery he stopped abruptly, and his hand on my elbow closed tightly. I glanced up. Something was moving toward us out of the deep shadow. The moonbeams dancing through the vines made a sudden arabesque of what looked to me for an instant like a great silver bell. It swung forward, rhythmic and graceful, and emerged into the broad wash of moonlight, lengthening at its top into the slender column of a waist and shoulders and a pale-gold-tipped head, with a crimson rose still in the high-piled coronet of glistening curls.

Anne Drayton came down the stairs. If I hadn't known her I would have thought she wasn't real—just something materialized ethereally out of the past, to deny modern functionalism and to confirm the reality of romance. And that's certainly what Steve thought. He stood staring at her with his mouth open a little. His hand relaxed and dropped to his side. She came down another step, looking at him.

"It's Mr. Heywood, isn't it?" she asked, without waiting for me to pull myself together and introduce them. "I'm Anne Drayton."

He stood stupidly staring at her, inarticulate, I imagine, for the first time in his life.

"I hoped you would come," she went on quietly. I hadn't noticed her voice before, or maybe it hadn't before had the quality it had now. Its soft native cadence was low and rich with the same intensity smoldering in her extraordinary eyes that were like black lakes of pitch.

"My cousin Lawrence told me you were an impossible bounder," she said, just as quietly. "I didn't believe him. I want to thank you for proving he was right. I should always have thought we were being unjust to you."

Steve straightened up. The calm contempt in her voice

was like a lash across his face.

"Your cousin Lawrence told me you were cross-eyed," he said coolly. "I can see why, of course. I'm happy to have proof, if I needed any, that he's a liar as well as a—"

She broke in on him, her eyes blazing but her voice perfectly even.

"I should have thought you'd already been offensive enough this evening, Mr. Heywood, without adding untruth to boorishness. You wouldn't dare say that to my cousin's face, just as you hadn't courage to say to mine what you said tonight. But that isn't what I waited out here to tell you. What I want to say to you is quite simply that you're more than welcome to the property you came here for, without the obligation that I assure you is infinitely more distasteful to me than it could possibly be to you. I don't want the Heywood estate, or any part of it. I've never understood Mr. Minot leaving it to me, except that I was devoted to him and he was a lonely old man. It seemed to me my proposal that we liquidate the estate and divide it evenly was fair under the circumstances, but I can now understand your ignoring it and standing on a legal technicality to get all of it. It was quite unnecessary, Mr. Heywood, If you'll tell me where you are staying, my uncle will come tomorrow and settle the whole thing— with the greatest of pleasure. If you'd been civil enough to come here in the first place, you'd have saved yourself the trouble of being so clever."

He just stood there, looking at her.

"Where are you staying, Mr. Heywood?" she repeated coolly.

"I'm—at Tangiers," he said. He took a step forward. "Look, Miss Drayton—"

"Good-by, Mr. Heywood."

She gathered her hoops lightly in her fingers. "Are you coming, Louise?"

I said, "Good night, Steve," and held out my hand. He

didn't even see it. He was looking at Anne, moving gracefully as a bit of thistledown across the gallery to the front door. I went up after her. She didn't so much as glance back. I did. He was still standing there, looking like some one whose hands were suddenly empty. Anne closed the door.

"I would suggest, Louise, that you go right up without bothering to say good night to my aunt and uncle tonight," she said quietly. "They're very much upset. I'll see you in the morning."

She went through the hall with me to the foot of the stairs.

"Good night," I said.

"Good night, Louise."

I went up. At the turn in the landing I glanced back down. She was standing there, her hand resting on the mahogany banister, looking in front of her, but not at anything that was there that I could see.

Chapter Six

THERE WAS A PINK NEWSPAPER lying on the marble-topped table in my room with a note on top of it. I picked it up. It was from Anne.

This is an old edition that came out when Antigua was open for the Pilgrimage, I read, *but I thought you might like to see it.*

I picked up the paper. It was a supplement devoted to the Garden Club Pilgrimage, and had pictures of houses on the Tour, with an historical sketch of each of them. I glanced through it, and stopped on the third page. Two houses were pictured there. Antigua was one of them. The other, and the one that had caught my attention, was Tangiers. *Separated by a deep bayou, Antigua and Tangiers, homes respectively of the Draytons and the Heywoods, stand back to back, though scarcely visible to each other through the lacy curtain of luxurious foliage.*

Tangiers, I thought; that was where Steve had said he was staying, and it must obviously be the house I'd seen through the trees across the bayou bristling with its arsenal of Spanish dagger and wired like No Man's Land with tangled vines and creeper.

I read on.

Both houses are famous in the history of Natchez. Natchez is full of stories of romance and bitterness that have grown up through more than a century in which the bayou has been the scene of adventures carefully concealed by the participants and discussed in whispers over the tea-cups in candle-lit drawing-rooms. It has been said that when the Union officers occupied Antigua at the invitation of the present occupants' grandfather to save it from destruction, a lovely lady whose portrait still hangs over the parlor mantel at Tangiers used to meet a young captain there secretly, unknown to her mother—who bolted Tangiers, kept iron wash boilers full of whale oil in the dining-room and parlor, and threatened to burn it to the ground if a Union soldier set foot in its hallowed precincts.

Lawrence Drayton, the father of the present owner of Antigua, was in the Confederate Army. He crept back one night to see the lovely daughter of Tangiers, whom he had left with many whispered vows. Finding her at her secret tryst with the dashing young captain, he drew his sword —and they say the eglantine winds luxuriantly out of the earth stained with the crimson tide of the Union officer's heart's blood. It is said that the coolness which marks the relations between Antigua and Tangiers also grew from that tragic episode. At any rate, the War ended, and the daughter of Tangiers married a distant cousin, also named Heywood, and the young Confederate married an heiress from Louisville, Ky. Notice the Chaperone's chair at Antigua and the tin bathtub in the bedroom at Tangiers. Both houses are closed on Sunday.

I put the paper down. Coolness between the two families seemed to me a definite understatement of the relations existing between them almost seventy-five years later. And it seemed a long time to keep the embers smoldering. Anne had said she'd been devoted to Minot Heywood, so the old fires must have died out at least between a very young girl and the lonely old man. He must have thought that by marrying her and Steve he would heal an old wound. That, I thought, must be the great wrong he had been talking about in his will, not whatever wrong he might have done to his cousin, Steve's father.

I heard Cornelia and Miss Letty come up the stairs and say good night in the hall. I looked at my watch. It was a little after eleven, and in spite of the fact that we'd got up at the crack of dawn to start the last of our journey along the Natchez Trace, I never felt less like going to bed in my life. Nevertheless, I undressed and climbed up into the great Victorian bed with its massive headboard, presided over by two smiling mahogany cherubs, their middles discreetly concealed by the ribbons by which they held aloft a basket of fruit and flowers, all carved in high relief. I turned out the light and lay there, looking at the path of the moonlight slanting across the gallery through the long open window.

It seemed to be drawing me out of the heavy bed with a kind of eerie fascination. I lay there a few moments longer, listening to the strange muted sounds that creep back into the world when the blatancy of day has died. Then I got up, slipped on my dressing-gown, opened the screen quietly, and went out on the gallery.

The broad lawns looked as if a heavy frost had fallen since I'd stood there earlier. The white azaleas and the dogwood were drifted snow outlining it. Across the bayou I could see Tangiers, a light shining in a single window in the upper gallery. The same moon had shone when the lovely daughter crept through the gardens to keep her tryst with the dashing captain, I thought, and I shivered a little. Women must have been braver in those days. There were too many black shadows flowing out like stationary pools of ink around the trees and shrubs. He must have been dashing indeed for a girl to have gone into the pitchy gash of the bayou—and it couldn't have been very difficult for her forsaken lover to conceal himself there, with not even a moonbeam filtering through to give him away.

I looked back to the garden below me. The light on the polished leaves of the giant magnolia made it look as if it were in blossom. A single firefly moved in the black ring at its base. I watched its tiny bright globe, thinking it was a little early for fireflies, and rather late at night for them, too. It was odd, the way it moved, glowing more brightly a moment, and down again, still glowing, always describing the same brief arc. All the fireflies I'd ever watched seemed to me to glow on their upward flight.

And then abruptly I realized that it wasn't a firefly at all. It was too red and too constant and its arc too stationary. It was a cigarette. I watched it intently for a moment. It seemed a curious thing for any one to be doing. If it was Lawrence or the Judge, or one of the colored boys, out in the garden, they'd hardly be standing under a tree when there were iron benches along the paths, and the glory of the night was the silver moon, not its shadows as murky as lampblack. Unless—I thought—there was a purpose behind it; unless whoever it was was there watching for something.

I realized, too, that I was plainly visible up there on the gallery in the pale phosphorescent light. If it was a secret watch, the man down there must be aware that I could see the glow of his cigarette. I was suddenly aware that the cigarette was gone. I heard a soft crackle of dry leaves, and silence. The man had just become aware of me; he'd dropped the cigarette and ground it out with his foot.

I was frightened, all of a sudden. I could feel a pair of eyes raised in the dark, watching me. It was in my imagination, I suppose, because scientists say there's no such thing as thought transference, but I had the creepy and rather terrifying feeling that there was something sinister there, and that those eyes I couldn't see, fastened on me, were narrowed and sharply malevolent.

I moved quickly. As I did I heard the dry brown leaves crackle again, and then in the stretch of frosted lawn before the next inky pool I saw a squat, swiftly moving shadow that wasn't human and didn't look like an animal. Then I saw the figure that cast the shadow. It was a man running doubled-up, like a football player. He streaked, absolutely noiseless, into the shadow of an evergreen, and out again into the light, and across the lawn to the drive and out of my sight.

I stood motionless, listening for the sound of the door closing. I don't know why I should have been so sure it was Lawrence Drayton, but I must have been. I certainly had no impulse to shout out and rouse the household.

Then I heard a car start up suddenly, and a motor racing violently for an instant. It seemed to come from a distance, outside the iron gates. Without being really conscious that I was doing it, I must have turned around, because I was abruptly aware of the single light shining across the dark sunken barrier of the bayou. That's the way I knew, however reluctantly I was forced to it, that I must already have realized who the silent watcher under the magnolia really was.

I don't know how long I must have stood there looking across the bayou. I only know that suddenly I saw two long fingers of light reach through the trees, and heard the hollow distant barking of dogs as the car came into the grounds of Tangiers and stopped. As the headlights went off, the barking changed to sharp high-pitched yelps of delight, and then there was silence. In a few minutes the single light in the gallery went off. An eerie brooding calm settled over the landscape, and the muted night noises crept out again.

"But it couldn't be Steve!" I whispered to myself. "He wouldn't do that sort of thing!"

It was almost as if a second self was answering me.

"How do you know what he'd do—or why? You never laid eyes on him until today. Instinct? Intuition? But maybe Cornelia's are sounder than yours. She didn't think very much of him. Or Lawrence, who knows him. Or Anne."

I went slowly back into my room. It was just the beginning of an argument between Faith and Doubt. Faith was much stronger, mostly. But Faith isn't always necessarily sound, and it can lead one pretty far afield at times.

I turned on the light, poured out a glass of water, and stood there drinking it, not because I was thirsty but because I had to translate a kind of emotional shock into some kind of energy to rid myself of it. I put down the glass and had started to climb into bed again when I heard a faint tap at my door, and saw the knob turn slowly and Cornelia's face in the resulting crack. And that was a shock in itself. She looked like a prospector who'd come unexpectedly on a hidden cache of gold. She came in quickly, closed the door and tiptoed across the room with an unholy gleam of delight in her eye.

"My dear," she whispered, glancing back at the door. She was still dressed in her black velvet period costume—though what period I've never known, having seen it do duty in receiving lines from the Daughters of Magna Carta to the Pageant of Tomorrow, through Colonial Dames and Daughters of the Revolution and of 1812 and tonight at the ante-bellum candlelight ball, and always looking as if it were quite authentic.

"My dear!" she repeated. She came over to the bed, glanced at the window, and went over and closed it. "I've just heard the most extraordinary thing! I'm not sure I even ought to repeat it to you!"

"What is it?" I asked.

"Promise not to breathe it to a living soul?"

I knew from experience she'd tell everybody she met until she found a more interesting item to take its place. But I nodded.

"After I came up with Letty and Anne, I remembered I hadn't told Millicent and Cora something, so I went back down to phone to them," she said. "And, my dear! The Draytons were in the dining-room having supper. People seem to eat at the most peculiar hours. There was a cold turkey and ham and salad and a bottle of wine, and the coffee smelled divine."

"Were they eating it secretly in the dark?"

"Don't be stupid, Louise," she said tartly. "I'm just telling you because that's why I happened to hear what I did. I had a sandwich at a roadside inn—just a service station, really—and I was starved, so I thought I'd go in and they'd ask me to sit down."

"I wouldn't have counted on it," I said.

"Louise! That's very discourteous, when we've forced our way in the way we have. And anyway, I didn't go in. I was just thinking about going in when I heard Judge Drayton say, 'If you can't hold your tongue, you ought to leave town till I've settled this. If you'd married her at Christmas as I begged you to, this would never have happened.' My dear, he was livid! Simply livid! All I could see was the back of his neck, but that was enough."

Cornelia began to take the pins out of her hair.

"And then Lawrence said, 'I can't *make* her marry me—not with you constantly harping that she mustn't suspect anything.' He was angry too. I don't like to say it, but I thought he was a little—well, you know what I mean. I'm not saying he was intoxicated, but I mean—"

"I know," I said.

"He said, 'I don't see why in blank—he said something else—you don't just tell her right out that she's—' And his father said, 'Stop it, this instant!' He was very angry. Lawrence said, 'Well, there you go again. When I marry her, by blank, I'll tell her. She's not going to—' And Judge Drayton cut him off just like that. 'You can tell her anything you like after you marry her, but not before. I should think you'd have learned something about women by this time. You can bulldoze some of them, but Anne's not one of them. Sometimes I wish she was my child instead of you. If it weren't for the press of circumstances, I wouldn't let her marry you.' And Lawrence fairly shouted, my dear! 'Yes, you'd rather have a—' His father said, 'Silence!' He didn't raise his voice, but it was just like thunder! Lawrence shut up like an oyster. 'I'm telling you you're behaving like an underbred puppy, and if you continue you'll have us in the poorhouse. We'd be there now if it weren't for your Aunt Kate and your Cousin Anne. Now listen to me. I'll attend to young Heywood. All you're required to do is keep Anne out of his way. I don't care how you do it. Take her to New Orleans, or out to look over the plantation—anything to keep her from talking to him. Do you understand that, or do I have to make it plainer?' "

Cornerlia shook out her hair and ran her fingers through it.

"Well, my dear, you should have heard Lawrence. He said, 'Yes, sir,' just as meek as Moses. Miss Drayton hadn't opened her mouth. I didn't even know she was in the room till she said, 'Your father's right, Lawrence. I'm afraid we won't get any cooperation from Laetitia. I think you'd better speak to her, Brother. And that young woman that's with her—Mrs. Gould. I think she's very dangerous.' And, my dear, I wouldn't repeat what the Judge said. I don't think he likes you very much."

"I imagine not," I said.

"Well, he would if he knew you, my dear," Cornelia said kindly. "I'm afraid you don't always make the effort you should. Anyway, what *do* you suppose it's all about? Who *is* this young Heywood?"

"He's the young man that's been following us," I said.

"You said his name was Maxwell."

"No. That's what you said."

"Why, Louise! I heard you very plainly. I never make mistakes with names. I've trained myself *very* carefully. Well, that explains it. No wonder he's going around under an assumed name. I don't blame Judge Drayton in the least."

She looked at her wrist. "I've left my watch in the car again!" she exclaimed. "It's standing right out there in the drive."

"Shall I go get it for you?"

"Oh, no, it's insured. I really wouldn't mind losing it. I just don't want it ripped off my wrist by brigands like young Maxwell. And by the way, Louise, have you noticed something?"

"A lot of things," I replied. "What in particular?"

"Letty's locket."

Cornelia lowered her voice to a whisper.

"She didn't have it on tonight. I asked Miss Drayton if it was an heirloom and she said she'd never heard of it. *I* believe Letty's hiding it."

"I wouldn't be surprised," I said. "I'd let it alone if I were you."

"I don't know what you're talking about, Louise," Cornelia said. "You're not implying that I go snooping about in things that don't concern me, I hope, my dear."

"Heavens, no," I said. "I was just afraid you might think perhaps it did concern you."

"Well, I think you must be tired, Louise. Good night."

She started for the door.

"Oh, by the way, Millicent and Cora are literally green. I told them we were stopping at Antigua, and they *nearly* died, my dear. They're paying eight dollars a day apiece and have to use the family bath and don't even get breakfast. They have to go down to the hotel. The house is picturesque and there's a quaint old chatelain, but they couldn't be more uncomfortable."

Cornelia smiled happily.

"They're staying at a place called Tangiers."

She glanced at the door.

"I think perhaps I might go back along the gallery. I have an idea one of them may have heard me, down there. You know how these old steps are."

I was to wonder for several days whether or not that precaution wasn't very fortunate, indeed, for me.

Chapter Seven

DANGEROUS DISCOVERY

As CORNELIA AND I were leaving Antigua the next morning to do the tour of the old houses, Anne came out of the drawing-room. Lawrence was just behind her.

"I've told you why I won't go," she was saying patiently. "It's sweet of you to ask me, but I *promised*. They're counting on me."

She smiled at us.

"Good morning. I hope our ghost didn't bother you. He roams around in the garden wearing a Union cap and tripping over his saber. What's the matter, Louise? Did you see him?"

"No," I said. "I slept too soundly."

It did come as a little shock to me nevertheless.

"Lawrence wants me to go over to the plantation to see about the ploughing with him," she said. "He's sulking because I promised I'd help receive at Melrose."

She turned back to him.

"Anyway, I promised I'd take Aunt Letty around this morning. She's going to be here only a couple of days, and I don't think we ought to run off for one of them."

"We wouldn't be gone all day," Lawrence said, rather shortly.

Anne laughed. "I've heard that before. Something always happens. Anyway, I'm in these clothes, and it's too much work getting out and in again."

She looked simply charming. She had on a brown alpaca gown with the same wide hoops but a snugly fitting bodice with long tight sleeves and a demure turned-over collar with a big cameo pin at her throat. Her hair was still piled in its shining coronet of curls on top of her lovely head, and she looked for all the world like an irrepressible little girl playing schoolmarm.

"You'd better wipe that lipstick off," I said. "Whoever wore that dress never even heard of it."

"And probably died an old maid as a result," she said gaily. She turned to Lawrence. "Why don't you come to Melrose?"

"To hear a lot of visiting firemen say their Aunt Susie has a chair just like that and a museum offered them a thousand for it? No, thanks."

"Don't be rude," Anne said sweetly. She smiled at us. "And don't you wear yourselves out, will you?"

In the car Cornelia looked at me.

"I think some one should warn that girl," she said. "I don't like that young man's looks. I wish Alec was here. She's the kind of girl I'd like *him* to marry. I wonder—"

"I'm rooting for Steve Heywood," I said. It was wonderful, I thought, what a good night's sleep will do for me. Now that morning was here, and the one glory of the sun had taken the place of the other glory of the moon—though why the burial service should have occurred to me when I was supposedly thinking about matrimony I don't know—I'd convinced myself that Steve had no doubt had a very good and adequate reason for skulking around the lawns of Antigua like one of Cornelia's common brigands. And anyway, maybe it wasn't Steve. Maybe it *was* the ghost of the dashing captain. I hadn't thought of that as a possible explanation, and I doubt if the captain could have done the line-plunging I'd seen the night before.

"You mean Maxwell," Cornelia said. "I don't think that would be suitable at all."

We let it go at that, and it wasn't until late that afternoon, when I was exhausted and Cornelia, as fresh as a daisy in her period gown, was again assisting her hostess, that Steve's name bobbed up again.

Melrose is one of the most beautiful and perfect places

I've ever seen. Miss Letty and I had come together with Lusby driving us. The pond with its elaborate screen of young green, the four stately white columns of the portico, and the simple gracious doorway, didn't entirely prepare me, even after Antigua and half a dozen other Victorian places we'd already done, for its really handsome and perfect interior. Nor, of course, for the shock of seeing Cornelia at the barrier across the back parlor saying, "We who love Natchez think Melrose is its own crowning jewel."

She saw me and put out her hand.

"Louise," she whispered. She had that don't-look-now-but intensity in her eye. "He's here again. I think it's Anne he's following now. You'd better warn her, and warn her to keep her eye on things. And Louise—I have something to tell you. I'll be through in a few minutes. This must be about the last batch. Be sure and tell Anne."

I glanced along the wide hall, like Antigua's only much larger, with the library on the same side as the double parlors. Steve Heywood was standing there propping up the door frame, his hand in his jacket pocket, as much at home as Cornelia herself. He had on a rough Irish tweed sports coat, worn but very good—the kind of thing a man likes and wears until he dies or his wife gives it to the Salvation Army—and a pair of gray flannel trousers and thick-soled English shoes. He was as casual as a house detective, and not really in the least like a burglar disguised as a Pilgrim with his eye on the family plate. In fact his eye was very definitely somewhere else, and he was listening with elaborate seriousness to the description of the contents of the room.

Behind him, coming just under his shoulder, was Cornelia's friend Millicent—Mrs. J. Philander Storm, I'd learned at lunch—and not far from her was Cornelia's friend Cora—Mrs. Samuel Johnson. I moved back a little to where I could see the hostess. It was Anne Drayton. She was telling the group about a candle shield on the mahogany desk in the corner. There was a bright pink spot on each cheek, and a smolder in her eyes that looked as if it could easily blaze up any minute. She was obviously going through her piece automatically, and all her conscious efforts were bent on ignoring the large tweedy presence leaning against the door. She finished about the candle shield and came back toward me.

Millicent, or probably I should say Mrs. Storm, leaned over the cord across the doorway and pointed to the table in the center of the room. I knew what she was going to say, of course.

"I have a table just like that," she announced. "A man from the Metropolitan Museum in New York offered me ten thousand dollars for it, but I wouldn't take it. I'm sorry I didn't, now."

She put her hand out and touched Anne's dress.

"I have a whole trunk full of old dresses like that in my attic being eaten up by moths. But I must say, my dear, you look simply lovely in it. It's very flattering, isn't it, Cora?"

Cora said yes it was.

"Do you suppose," Steve remarked blandly, "that they're as beautiful in sweaters and skirts?"

Mrs. Storm looked critically at Anne, as if she were a wax model instead of a girl.

"I think sports clothes are more for the Northern or Western type," she said. "Of course, *anybody's* attractive in costume, I always think."

"Possibly," Steve said judicially. "But with eyes and voices like those they have here it really doesn't matter."

The two spots in Anne's cheeks were a brilliant scarlet.

"I beg your pardon, miss," Steve said, "but what did you say the bookcases were made of?"

The Pilgrims were moving away.

"Mahogany," Anne said, with exasperated calm, "for the sixth time in the last ten minutes. And now if you don't mind will you please go on to another house?"

"I'm interested only in Melrose," Steve said amiably.

"Then please move along to another room so somebody else can see something."

"But I'm interested only in libraries."

"It was dining-rooms a while ago," Anne said icily.

"It's libraries now." He couldn't have been more imperturbable. "By the way, did I tell you my Aunt Selina has a desk just like that?"

"And the Metropolitan offered her a hundred thousand dollars for it, I suppose."

Millicent and Cora had gone out through the back gallery to the dairy house.

"No, that was her table like the one in the dining-room," Steve said. "The desk was two hundred thousand."

A quick smile flashed in her eyes and was gone instantly.

"She wouldn't take it, of course," she said coolly.

Steve grinned.

"Right. But she's sorry now."

In the novels of the period for which she was dressed Anne would have tapped her little foot impatiently on the floor. She didn't now, but the effect was the same.

"You know, Mr. Heywood," she said, with icy sweetness, "I think you ought to be very much interested in the parlor furniture too. I'm sure your Aunt Selina wouldn't want you to miss it. Wouldn't you like to step inside?"

"I'd be charmed—Miss Drayton, I believe, isn't it?"

She unhooked the cord across the door and held it aside. As he went in, she stepped back and hooked it across again.

"Mrs. Cartwright!" she called.

Cornelia, resting a moment on the brocatelle sofa just through the great double doors, rose blossoming graciously.

"Hey!" Steve whispered. "This is a foul trick!"

"This gentleman is an interior decorator, Mrs. Cartwright," Anne said. "He's *so* interested. He's been around for hours. Won't you show him the parlors?"

Cornelia took one look at Steve. Her lips tightened. "Oh," she said. "Mr. Maxwell."

Anne looked surprised for an instant. "Do keep him a long time," she said. "Good-by, Mr.—?"

"Heywood," said Steve pleasantly. "Good-by, Miss Drayton."

I don't know why I hadn't realized I wasn't the only interested person looking on. I did then, just as Anne turned with a smile flickering in her eyes and in the corners of her red lips. Judge Drayton had come in through the back gallery and was standing in the door, very definitely not amused.

He took a step forward. "Anne," he said.

"Oh, Uncle Ed! I thought Lawrence was coming for me."

She slipped her arm through his affectionately.

"Uncle Ed." Her voice sobered. "Did you talk to Mr. Heywood today about—"

"I've asked you to leave all that to me, Anne," Judge Drayton said quietly. "Run along and get your things, and hurry like a good girl. Your Aunt Kate isn't well. I'm afraid you're going to have to take her to New Orleans to the doctor in the morning."

"Oh, dear!" Her voice fell, and I saw her uncle glance at her sharply. "I'm sorry," she said. "I didn't mean that. Of course I'll take her. I won't be a minute."

She ran upstairs. Judge Drayton came over to where I was examining the famous table whose inlaid emeralds and rubies the Northern soldiers had picked out and taken away.

"Our attempts to protect our jewels haven't always been successful, you see, Mrs. Gould," he said evenly.

"But the attempt has always been valiant," I replied.

He gave me a wintry smile.

"I think one may say so," he answered softly.

I didn't see them leave. I was looking around the house. The Pilgrims were slowly clearing out to the dairy house and kitchen, and the front door was closed.

Cornelia came out of the drawing-room.

"I don't think that young man has ever been in a civilized house before," she said crossly. "And by the way, I'm staying to supper. But before you leave—"

She fished around in her needle-point bag.

"I think we ought to clear up our accounts as we go. Here's yours. It includes your lunch today and a ten-cent tip for the waitress. I've pro-rated Lusby's pay and divided it up between the three of us, as well as his food and lodging. I think that's fair. We've all used his services."

I took the bill she handed me. I don't know why it should have annoyed me. I certainly meant to pay my share, and I knew Cornelia's habits where money was concerned. I didn't even mind paying a dollar a day toward Lusby's wages, because she'd never paid her servants well anyway. I suppose it was being handed the bill just then instead of later in my room.

"I haven't any money with me," I said. "I'll pay you tonight."

"Oh, anytime," Cornelia said. "I just don't want to run short."

For a really very rich woman, Cornelia hated to cash a check worse than any one I've ever known.

"Was that what you wanted to tell me?" I asked.

"Oh, no." She looked around quickly. "My dear, it's about Anne. I've found out all about what Lawrence meant. I'll tell you later. And Letty's locket—I've found out about that too. I saw a picture of it. She left her bag in the car, and the locket was in it, and I opened it. Ssssh! Here she comes. I'll tell you later."

I don't think I've ever been so furious in my life. I looked at Miss Letty, coming out of the dining-room with a lovely woman in a handsome taffeta dress of about 1880.

Her gentle face was flushed and she looked very pleased. I bit off the words that crowded to my tongue.

"Oh, Letty dear," Cornelia said. "Lusby will take you and Louise home. I'm staying on."

"But—I've been asked to stay too," Miss Letty said, a little frightened, I thought, that Cornelia wasn't going to allow it.

"That's very nice, I'm sure," Cornelia said stiffly. "Lusby can take you, Louise. Be sure he's back in time for me to change."

I went out on the front gallery, still boiling mad. If I had to walk back, Lusby wasn't going to take me. As I started down the steps I saw Steve sitting there in his old car.

"Hullo," he said. "I've been waiting for you. What about having some chow with me?"

"I'd love it," I said.

He looked at me curiously. "What's the matter?"

"Nothing. Just all the things I didn't have a chance to say to Cornelia Cartwright."

I'm very glad, now, that I didn't say them, for that was the last time I saw Cornelia Cartwright alive. Incredible as it was, some time between the hour that I was eating catfish and mustard greens with Steve Heywood at the hotel and the end of the Miracle Play at the colored church where Anne and I were saving a seat that she never came to occupy, Cornelia disappeared. When they found her she was dead. The bayou that slashed between Tangiers and Antigua was stained crimson with her blood, as it had been stained with the heart's blood of the dashing captain three-quarters of a century ago. They had found her, and they had sent for her stepson to come from New Orleans, before Anne and I got back to Antigua at midnight.

Chapter Eight

Vanishing Pilgrim

I suppose one of the curious things about the murder of Cornelia Cartwright was that nobody wanted to talk about it—I mean, none of the local people I met. Not to an outsider, anyway, although Cornelia, of course, was an outsider herself. They certainly talked about it among themselves. When I came into Connelly's Tavern the first time after it happened, the women there all stopped talking abruptly and busied themselves with anything else like a lot of bird dogs.

And it wasn't because it ruined the Pilgrimage. It made it, as far as numbers were concerned. There never were as many people in Natchez, not since its last *cause célèbre;* and a great many "nice" people came too, since they had the excuse of the Pilgrimage, who wouldn't have dreamed of rushing in on that other occasion. If Antigua had taken down its *Closed* sign, and Tangiers hadn't barred the entrance and removed the Garden Club's green arrows, they could have made more money than all the Indian Mounds and Devil's Punch Bowls around town put together. Since people couldn't get to the bayou they went to the old houses instead, hoping to pick up a morsel or two of gossip along with the culture. And it wasn't altogether dignity or decency that made the local people not talk about it either, though there was a lot of that, too. There was something else that I couldn't quite put my finger on. The nearest I've been able to come to it is a sort of clannishness, though what Lawrence Drayton said may be nearer the truth.

"There's a kind of tacit blackmail in towns like this," he said. "Too many people have skeletons in their own closets.

There's always the danger that if you start to talk, I'll talk too."

For a moment I thought he meant me and himself. It gave me a little shock until I realized he was using us as impersonal pronouns. And whether he was right or not, the fact was that everybody was singularly mum when I came around, at Connelly's Tavern and elsewhere.

I've pieced together from what Miss Letty and Lusby told me what happened before Cornelia left the house. What happened afterward wasn't so simple, because nobody knew. I don't pretend, of course, that I'm certain either Miss Letty or Lusby told me the whole, unvarnished truth, but for what it's worth this is what they told me:

Cornelia and Miss Letty came back to Antigua about half past seven. They were going to pick up Millicent (Mrs. Storm) and Cora (Mrs. Johnson) at Tangiers, and take them to the spirituals at the colored church. The Draytons were all going because their cook was in the choir and Mamie, the housemaid, was in the miracle play. She was the pert young hussy the Devil tempted gaily along the primrose path who wound up weeping in a wonderfully realistic hell while the angels in heaven sang for joy. Miss Kate, however, was indisposed and didn't come, and Lawrence and the Judge stayed briefly, just long enough, in fact, to show Steve Heywood that Anne was carefully guarded. When he left, they did too. They were to pick me and Anne up at the end, and it was on account of Cornelia that they didn't. That's how it happened that Steve and Anne and I had coffee together—though at the present time that, as the mid-Victorian novel would say, is another story.

The Draytons, except Miss Kate, left Antigua a little after half past seven. Lawrence and his father had to stop by the office for something, and Anne waited in the drugstore on Main Street, talking to a member of the Garden Club.

Cornelia came down to the library about a quarter to eight. Miss Letty was there (in her account) reading a book, and told Cornelia she was tired and had decided not to go. Cornelia was annoyed. When Miss Letty was adamant, she went out and told Lusby to go after the two ladies at Tangiers and pick her up after he'd collected them. Lusby agreed she was definitely provoked about something. He started off at once. Cornelia went back to the library, phoned Tangiers and explained that Lusby was on his way over. She then started to argue with Miss Letty again, insisting it was her duty to go. Miss Letty was determined not to go—though how she'd mustered courage to stand up to Cornelia I wouldn't know. The phone rang, and Cornelia answered it.

The conversation, Miss Letty said, was very brief. The end of it she could hear went like this:

"This is Mrs. Cartwright speaking."

Cornelia then said, "Oh," in her flat uncompromising tone, as if she wasn't pleased but wasn't particularly surprised. She said then, "If you have anything you want to tell me, there's plenty of other opportunity to do it right here." She listened an instant and said. "Very well, but I don't want to be late. I've agreed to bring the Northern visitors' greetings to the colored people after the spirituals are over, and I wouldn't care to disappoint them."

That was perfect Cornelia, of course. She always managed to bring greetings wherever she went. In fact I've never seen a program she wasn't on in such a capacity if not also several others. When they were questioning Miss Letty, Alec Cartwright said she must be telling the truth because it was too perfect, she couldn't possibly have made it up. I don't know, of course. It's like saying Helen Hokinson must be president of a garden club. Many times I've thought Miss Letty was brighter than she looked or acted, and that Cornelia didn't entirely fool her even if she never let on.

Then, according to Miss Letty, Cornelia put on her gloves and started out. Miss Letty went to the front door with her and saw the car drive up. She then closed the door and went back to the library to read her book and listen to the news over the radio—and that's the last she saw of Cornelia.

Lusby and one of the two ladies said that Miss Letty closed the door. Mrs. Philander Storm (Millicent) said she slammed it. Lusby hadn't noticed that, and Mrs. Johnson (Cora) said it was her impression that she didn't close the door at all but left it ajar, which is why she assumed Mrs. Cartwright was returning to the house. They all agreed that Cornelia came down the steps, leaned in the car and said, "You'd better let Lusby take you along. I'm going to be a little late, but I'll join you at the church. My friend Miss Anne Drayton has asked me especially to sit with her, but I dare say you'll be able to find seats in the back somewhere. And I'll take you home after the concert."

Lusby closed the door then, and Cornelia went back up on the gallery—and that was the last they saw of her. Miss Letty said she didn't come into the house. She didn't hear a shot, furthermore, but it was a chilly night; the doors and windows were closed, and anyway she was listening to the radio. Miss Kate Drayton thought she had heard something, but she didn't notice it because she was in bed with a witch-hazel poultice over her eyes, suffering with migraine, and her windows were closed to keep out the miasma that affected her sinuses. If she had heard it, which she wasn't sure about, she must have assumed it was a car backfiring in Albermarle Street. Mamie's beau had a car that sounded like Christmas firecrackers. She hadn't seen her sister, but supposed she was in the library reading and listening to the radio as she'd said.

They were alone in the house. All the servants left at four o'clock, as they did everywhere else in Natchez, except

Isaac who lived on the place; and he'd gone to the church to see Mamie in the play. They didn't have a dog. They had dogs on the plantation, but not in town, because it was impossible, with young people around, to keep them out of the house. She was sorry about Mrs. Cartwright. She'd seemed like a very pleasant woman, though she'd been too busy to give them the opportunity to enjoy her company as much as they would have liked.

From the time Cornelia left the car and started up onto the gallery, no one had the slightest idea of what had happened to her—except that something very awful had. It seemed reasonable that whoever had shot her and left her in the bayou was somebody known to her and whom she was not afraid of. If it was whoever had called her on the telephone, and if Miss Letty's account of that call was true —and there was no reason for any one to think it wasn't— then it was also someone she had no great enthusiasm about seeing. The one thing I was worried about, at the time, was that it wasn't like Cornelia not to have told Letty whom she was seeing—because silence about anything wasn't like her. She always made a point about how many demands were made on her time and who was making them.

At any rate, she didn't come to the church. I saw her two friends, Mrs. Storm and Mrs. Johnson. To spite her, I imagine, they'd taken front seats, until they saw the charming president of the local garden club and moved back with her.

"I wonder where Aunt Letty and Mrs. Cartwright are," Anne whispered to me. "Isaac and Mamie will be so disappointed if Miss Baby doesn't come."

She looked around. I saw her face flush as she turned back quickly. She was smiling a little in spite of herself. Judge Drayton and Lawrence were still with us, and the stage hands were having trouble with the lights. Every time Hell would get a beautiful glowing red, the lights in

Heavenly Jerusalem would go out, and vice versa. It was good religion but bad stagecraft.

"I wish you'd do something about your friend," she said.

I glanced back. Steve was standing by the door where I'd left him, as much at home there as he'd been at Melrose. It wouldn't have surprised me to have seen him up helping with the lighting. He grinned at me, shook his head with a sour glance at the Judge and Lawrence, and indicated in pantomime that he was leaving.

"He's gone now," I said to Anne.

"Good. I hope it's permanent."

"He's rather amusing, really," I remarked.

"So is a chimpanzee," she said. Then she smiled. "He's been on a lot of garden tours. I didn't realize at first he was pulling my leg. I thought he was just another of the tourists you wonder about—why they come if they have everything so much better at home."

She glanced back. I thought she looked a little sorry that he'd gone.

"Who *is* his Aunt Selina?" she asked.

I laughed. "I don't know. He probably just made her up out of whole cloth."

"What does he do?"

"I don't know that either. He's apparently on his way to Kelly Field. I gather he's a pilot among other things. Lawrence would know."

"And he'd have apoplexy if I asked him. He doesn't like him."

"It seems to be mutual," I remarked.

The lights were working at last. I forgot all about Steve and the rest of them in the really very moving and naïve play of the fight between St. Peter and the Devil, as Good and Evil, for the souls of men. Some of the voices were beautiful. I've never heard spirituals that seemed to me so naturally and feelingly sung. The Devil was a genuine comedian, trying to lure the sinners off the straight and narrow path down the side aisle of the little church. It was exciting, too. I was almost in tears when a mother in the heavenly choir clasped her wayward daughter, finally saved, in her arms. Mamie was wonderful, flirting her skirt and ogling the Devil, and I hoped Lusby was somewhere around to see her—or maybe I didn't. Or perhaps her wailing in Hell with its shadowy flames through the red isinglass windows was a lesson neither of them would disregard.

When the lights went on again, Judge Drayton and Lawrence had slipped out. I'd been so absorbed I hadn't noticed them leave. Anne looked around.

"It's funny," she said. "They must not have come. Aunt Letty and Mrs. Cartwright."

I looked too, but they weren't anywhere in the crowded room. We listened to the thanks of the president of the garden club and two other visitors, and left. At the door Anne shook hands with the preacher.

"It was splendid, Mr. Green."

"Thank you, Miss Anne," he said. "I'm sorry Miss Laetitia couldn't come. I hoped she'd say a few words to the audience."

"She'll come Friday," Anne said. "She had a very hard day."

"I'd certainly like to see her, Miss Anne."

"She said especially she wants to see you. Why don't you come out to Antigua sometime tomorrow?"

"I'd like to do that, Miss Anne."

We went on out.

I turned as someone spoke behind me. " 'Scuse me, please, Miss Louise."

Lusby was standing on the curb, his cap in his hand, obviously worried.

"What am Ah s'posed to do, miss? Ah cain' find Mis' Cartwright, no place. She said she'd be comin' along, but she never come, so Ah went back, but Ah cain' find her. She ain' at the house, an' Ah don' know where she gone to. It ain' like her not to be where they's a meetin' goin' on."

I smiled. "She was probably tired."

"No, ma'am. Mah madam she don' get tired. An' Ah been back twice, an' Miss Drayton ain' seen her since we lef'. Ah brung them two ladies—is Ah s'posed to take them back home?"

I nodded. "And then you go on home. Mrs. Cartwright will be there by this time, probably. Don't worry. She'll be all right."

"Yes, miss. Is you an' Miss Anne comin' too? Mr. Lawrence said if he didn' come back, you was to come with me. An' Ah ain' seen him around."

Anne took hold of my arm. "I think we'll walk, Lusby," she said.

He hesitated. "Mr. Lawrence he said Ah was to bring you back with me."

"That's all right," I said.

He still hesitated. "Miss Louise, do you s'pose Mis' Cartwright would mind if Ah come back an' take Mamie home —as long as you ain' comin'?"

"If she does, tell her I told you to," I said. "I'll explain it to her."

Lusby grinned. "Thank you, Miss Louise."

Anne and I walked up toward Main Street. It was a beautiful night. The moonlight touched the mean roadway and its tumbledown cottages with a silvery glamour heightened by the long-drawn hoooing of the whistle of some boat on the Mississippi.

"It's been ages since I walked home," Anne said. "And it isn't very far."

We came into Main Street. I don't know how long they've called it that, but it's a very good name for it. Even the pots of pink and white and red petunias hanging from the lamp posts put there by the Natchez Garden Club for the duration of this Pilgrimage couldn't do very much for it, though they helped. The efforts of certainly one of the most active and intelligent groups of club women in America couldn't keep down the garish canvas signs and white painted arrows of people trying to commercialize a fine and dignified civic undertaking after it had proved a successful one.

"Let's get some coffee," Anne suggested. "It isn't late." She smiled. "As long as we don't meet your friend, Mr. Heywood, I don't think Uncle Ed will mind."

We walked down the tawdry street lined with wooden store buildings that would make a pyromaniac go out of his mind and that contrasted so sharply with the stately public buildings and the gracious dignity of Rosalie, the Parsonage, and Ravenna of the days when cotton was king. There were a number of people in the coffee shop when we went in, but Steve was not among them. Maybe it was only human, or maybe it was just my imagination, but I thought Anne looked just a little disappointed. We sat down at the low counter.

"I haven't asked you how you like Natchez," she said with a smile. "You don't have to answer, because I really want to ask you something—about my Aunt Letty." Her face sobered. "Have you known her long?"

I shook my head. "We only came to Brentwood five years ago. I've known her since then. I'm very fond of her."

"So am I," Anne said. "I like her best, really. She took care of me mostly, after my parents were drowned in a hurricane off Jamaica. Aunt Letty came to Abbeville in Georgia, where they'd left me, and brought me here. I was just a year old, so I don't remember that, but she took care of me mostly until I was ten. Then she went to Brentwood. But what I wanted to ask is—is she very poor?"

She stirred her coffee, her head bent down so that her long shining bob, now that she wasn't in costume—and curiously enough was wearing a sweater and skirt—hung down around her chin.

"I mean—well, her underthings and her shoes—well, she doesn't look as if she had any money at all."

"I don't think she has very much," I said gently.

She looked at me. That odd sort of indignant look her face got was on it now.

"I don't see why not," she said. "I mean she ought to have plenty to live on comfortably. We do."

"Maybe she hoards it," I replied, "but I doubt it. Anyway, it doesn't follow that because you have money she has it."

She started to retort warmly, and stopped. Then she said calmly, "Something might have happened to it. She had the same as the others originally. Grandmother divided the estate that way. I have Father's share and Aunt Kate spends all her time studying the stock market reports. And I know a fourth of Antigua belongs to Aunt Letty, because they always have to have her signature. It annoys Uncle Ed, because she's never given him a power of attor—"

She stopped abruptly. She was looking past me at the door, and the color was rising in her cheeks. I glanced around. It was Steve, all right.

Chapter Nine

BODY IN THE BAYOU

"WELL," HE SAID, coming down the narrow aisle behind us. "I thought I'd missed you. Mind if I join you?"

"Not unless Miss Drayton does," I said. The only vacant seat was next to Anne.

"Do you always follow people around?" Anne asked.

Steve grinned.

"Only special people. It just happens I came in here for coffee, believe it or not. You can't get a drink decently in this town, and my speakeasy days are over. I didn't know there still were such places."

"There's an old Mississippi custom," Anne said. "We always stagger to the polls and vote dry."

"Now that's cynical, Miss Drayton. I'm surprised at you."

He sat down and looked at her critically.

"I'd never have known you with your pigtails, if it hadn't been for your bodyguard," he observed easily. "Isn't it way past your bedtime, sister?"

She looked at him blankly. As a matter of fact she didn't look a day over sixteen, with a little yellow bow on each side of her head to hold her curls back, and a yellow sweater under a perky green plaid suit with a flared skirt coming just below the knees. It was the first time he'd seen her in modern clothes, of course.

She smiled suddenly.

"Maybe if you put your hair up—"

"What for?" she demanded.

"Well, I don't want people to think I've adopted a war orphan—much less married one. Because I've decided to marry you."

"You have?" she asked politely. "You can't imagine how grateful I am."

"Don't mention it. As a matter of fact, it's not going to be nearly as tough as I thought it was."

"It's going to be a lot tougher," Anne said. "As a matter of fact, it's going to be absolutely impossible."

He looked at her with cool critical detachment.

"That's what *I* thought, last night," he agreed thoughtfully. "But today I think you're rather nice. Not impossible at all—with a few minor changes—like getting down off your high horse and getting rid of your family. Where shall we live? Any place you like just so it's Philadelphia."

Anne laughed.

"I guess I forgot to say it's you that's absolutely impossible," she replied calmly. "I don't suppose that ever occurred to you."

"Tut, tut," Steve said. "And by the way."

He fished around in his inside jacket pocket.

"Did you have your uncle write me this letter? Maybe I'd better read it to you."

He looked around. Only the three of us were left in the coffee shop, and the waitresses were at the other end of the counter. Anne had stiffened a little, and was sitting there straight as a young, gold-tipped arrow, a little flush rising in her cheeks.

He pulled a long envelope out of his pocket and opened it.

" 'Dear Mr. Heywood,' " he read. " 'My niece has informed me of her meeting with you last night. Distasteful as it was to her, she still feels that since she is unwilling to submit to the terms suggested by Minot Heywood in his will, it is only fair and honorable for a settlement to be made whereby an equitable division of the property may be effected. She has therefore suggested that, when you have reached your twenty-sixth birthday, she convey to you two of the six plantations—Argosy and Blenheim, lying in the country—and Tangiers in the city of Natchez, now occupied by Miss Rose Heywood. I am enclosing statements of the recent proceeds of the six plantations. You will see that the income from Argosy and Blenheim equals that of three of the estates she is retaining, and that the fourth has operated without profit for a number of years.

" 'I have strongly advised her against making any concessions at all, as the terms of the will are most definite. My niece's sense of fair play, and her natural very strong desire to rid herself of your unwelcome attentions, are all that persuades me to act in accordance with her wishes.' "

He folded the letter up and put it back in the envelope.

"Another cup of coffee, please. What about you, Louise?"

I nodded.

"Sister Anne?"

She shook her head automatically.

"He adds that this is without prejudice," Steve went on coolly, "and that the sooner I get out of town the quicker. That's South'n hospitality for you. But I've got a two-dollar ticket for the black arrow tour tomorrow, so I guess I'll have to disappoint him."

She looked at him, her eyes shining.

"I'm sorry my uncle was rude," she said. "But you'll admit you weren't very civil to him, or to me for that matter. And I don't see what's wrong with the rest of it. I think it's very fair. You certainly want to keep Tangiers, don't you? Even if you haven't any feeling about it yourself, your Cousin Rose hasn't any place else to live. And I thought you'd want the Heywood things in it. My uncle didn't want to make any compromise at all. He was furious. I insisted, because I thought it was the decent thing to do, and the fairest arrangement we could make."

Steve was examining his cigarette with sardonic imperturbability.

"Not really?"

"Yes, really!" she retorted hotly. "But now I take it you're going to insist on all or nothing. Is that it?"

"Oh, no," Steve said. "I just insist on marrying you, that's all. I think you're a *very* nice girl."

The corners of her lips were trembling, her eyes were blazing.

"May I see that letter, please?"

"What for?"

"I'd like to see if he wrote it the way you read it. Or if you made it up as you went along—the way you do your Aunt Selina."

He handed it to her with a grin. She glanced through it.

"Word for word, Mr. Heywood," she said lightly. "Well, if you're standing on your legal rights, I expect I'll have to do the same."

She tore the letter into a dozen pieces and stuffed them into her jacket pocket.

Steve watched her with sardonic amusement.

"That doesn't change anything," he said. His blue eyes twinkled irrepressibly. "I'm perfectly willing to do my part. I'll marry you. Any time you say."

She looked at him, calm outwardly and boiling inside.

"It would serve you right if I said okay, tomorrow at nine—except that I'll be gone by then. And anyway, I wouldn't marry you, Steve Heywood, if I had to be an old maid and die in the poorhouse, and you know it."

"Thanks a lot," Steve said.

She turned to me.

"Are you coming, Louise, or are you staying here?" she demanded hotly.

She was close to tears—of rage and futility. I didn't blame her. His cheerful and unruffled calm was maddening. As she stalked out to keep from flying at him, probably, and making a scene in front of the waitresses, I said, "I think you're a pig."

"Me, or somebody," he said. He looked at me oddly for an instant. "Is she going away?"

I nodded. "Her aunt's ill, apparently."

"That's interesting," he said. "Well, I'll be seeing you."

I went on out and joined Anne.

"I don't think I've ever hated anybody before in all my life," she said passionately. "I could have—oh, dear!"

I didn't say anything, and we walked along rather breathlessly in a sizzling silence.

"I guess Uncle Ed is right," she said. "He says the Heywoods have always been polecats. Skunks is what he said. I thought it was just because the two families never got along, but—"

She shrugged her slim shoulders and lapsed into silence again. Behind us the clock on the church tower struck twelve. Suddenly she gave a sort of reluctant little laugh.

"As a matter of fact," she said, "I'm not sure it wouldn't be fun—"

She stopped for a moment, and went on.

"I mean, I rather like him, really. There's something about him—"

She didn't say any more, and I didn't say anything. We walked on in the empty street. In front of us as we came along we could see the gates of Antigua. They were open, and beyond the trees we saw the house aglow from cellar to garret.

Anne drew a sharp quick breath.

"Oh, dear, they're probably scared to death! I'm not allowed out alone at night."

Steve was right, I thought; she was very young, and rather scared. But her chin was up.

"I shouldn't have stayed out, really," she said. "I've got to take Aunt Kate away for another cure in the morning. It's always the way—just when I don't want to leave. On account of the Pilgrimage, I mean."

I smiled. We were halfway up the drive. She stopped

abruptly again and caught hold of my arm.

"It's the doctor! Maybe Aunt Kate's really—"

Then her fingers closed tightly. "And the police! What's *happened?*"

She started running wildly toward the house. But it wasn't Miss Kate. They'd found Cornelia's body in the bayou.

Chapter Ten

INCREDIBLE PROPOSAL

MISS LETTY WAS on the front gallery. She let the brown wrapper she was holding tightly around her drop, put her arms around Anne and held her passionately, tears of relief coming to her eyes.

"Thank God you're safe," she whispered. She was more upset than I could ever have imagined her being.

We stood there bewildered.

"What *is* it?" Anne cried.

"If you'd been home, instead of traipsing about having us worried out of our minds, you'd know," Miss Kate Drayton said sharply. "Mrs. Cartwright has been killed. They found her body half an hour ago down in the bayou, after they'd searched everywhere for her. We didn't know *what* had happened to you."

I stared at her unable to believe my ears.

"Cornelia?" I gasped.

Miss Letty took my hand. "Yes, Louise," she said gently. "It's terrible. We've sent for Alec."

"But where—where is she?"

"Be calm, Louise," Miss Letty said. "They're doing everything they can. There's very little they can do. But we must be calm."

Her hand was trembling, and yet in a sense she was very calm indeed. Her voice was steady and low-pitched, as Anne's had been under the stress of emotion the night before.

"My head is splitting," Miss Kate said abruptly. "Anne, go get my smelling salts on my dressing-table. And take these."

She may have been ill, but she'd had time to do something about herself before she went to bed. Her iron-gray hair was in curling pins, and she had on a pink chin strap. She took it off now and held it out with the pins.

Anne was too stunned to move.

"Don't stand there," Miss Kate said. "Do as I ask you, at once."

"But—Mrs. Cartwright—"

"I know," said her aunt. "There's nothing you can do about it. Just why it had to happen here of all places. It seems to me an extraordinary breach of hospitality. It's the green bottle, not the purple one. And bring my coat. We'll catch our death of colds. Hurry, child."

Anne moved automatically into the house, her face pale, her eyes tragic and uncomprehending. Miss Kate turned to Miss Letty.

"You brought that woman here," she said angrily, drawing her pink chenille bathrobe tightly around her thin figure. She was tall and angular, cast in the same mold, though with harsher outlines, than her brother and all the side-whiskered gentlemen whose portraits hung throughout Antigua. She had the same dark Drayton eyes, only hers snapped fire and brimstone while her brother's were hard and shuttered. Of the three only Miss Letty's were like Anne's—and as Anne's had been, they were smoldering now with suppressed fire. It was curious, and I'd thought it before, how a family characteristic of the sort could take on such different qualities, depending on the individual's inner personality. The pride and confidence, arrogance even, of the two older Draytons was in such extraordinary contrast to the younger one's patient and almost wistful submissiveness. But that was wearing thin just then. Miss Letty's breath came quickly.

"You brought that woman here," Miss Kate repeated. "You—"

Miss Letty took two quick steps toward her sister.

"Stop it, Kate!"

Her voice was like a thin jet of steam escaping from impossible pressure.

"I've listened to all I'm going to from you tonight. Now stop it! Stop it, I say!"

Miss Kate took a step back, her mouth sagging, her eyes blank with amazement.

"And don't say anything else, not to me or to Anne or anybody. You've always been cruel and heartless. God will strike you! You can go on destroying the living, but God takes care of the dead. He won't allow you to go on being a brutal and selfish old woman.—And I give you and my brother an answer now, once and for all: Anne shall not marry Lawrence Drayton—not until I'm lying out there where Cornelia Cartwright is lying. And I warn you again that God will punish you—and you too, Edward —punish you both as you deserve, the rest of your lives! Do you hear me, Edward?"

Her brother had come up the gallery steps and was standing utterly aghast for an instant, staring at her turned miraculously into a flaming brand white-hot with passion. Then he made a swift move toward her, his eyes on the door.

"Go to your room, Anne—at once," he said curtly.

I turned. Anne was standing there, the little bottle of smelling salts in her hand. Miss Kate's coat had slipped off her arm and was lying on the floor. She was staring, blank-faced and frightened, at her aunt. Miss Letty turned, and stopped as if she had been struck suddenly dumb.

"Go, Anne!" her uncle repeated imperatively. "Go, I say. And you go inside, Laetitia." His voice was like steel, and so was his grip on her arm.

Miss Letty moved through the door, dazed and faltering. I started toward her. Judge Drayton's quiet gesture had so much authority that I stopped where I was.

"My sister is upset, Mrs. Gould," he said evenly. "She needs to be alone for a little while."

He turned to Kate Drayton, looking at her silently for a moment, his lips pressed together. "Go back to bed, Kate. I'll talk to you later. Has Lawrence come?"

Miss Kate didn't answer. She just stood looking at him. *She's afraid of him,* it flashed over me; *she's terribly afraid of him.*

"My son went to find Anne, Mrs. Gould," Judge Drayton said coolly, turning to me. "We were worried about her. I think you had better go inside, too. They will be bringing her around. It will be better if you are not present. The police will want to see you before they go."

At the door of the library I came to a startled halt. I don't quite know how to describe the impression I had of Miss Letty in the split second in which she flashed around to face me. A wounded animal at bay is part of it. She had obviously been so intent on watching something through the window and across the back gallery—and there was only one thing to watch out there—that she hadn't heard me in time to cover up. Even then I couldn't bring myself to put the other word to what I saw. Fear and defiance were there—and something else; and "surprise" was as far as I could go in thinking what it was.

Anyway, it was so brief I couldn't really be sure I'd seen it at all. It seemed to crumple right in front of me, and out of it Miss Letty herself emerged, tottering, shaken and uncertain, to the sofa. She sat there, her lips twitching in nervous spasms.

"I shouldn't have done what I did, Louise," she whispered. "I shouldn't have said that."

There were footsteps out in the hall.

"And Louise—don't let them arrest Lusby. That's the first thing they'll think of. Go out and see that they don't."

She got up unsteadily and almost pushed me out the door.

I went back down to the front gallery. The red taillight of a big black car was disappearing down the drive. Then

I saw Lusby. He was standing with three men by Cornelia's car—the color of putty, I knew—and they were trying to make him talk, and he couldn't. They were shooting one question after another at him. Where had he been? When had he seen her last? Where was the gun?

That seemed to bring him to some kind of life.

"In here," he said, and began tugging at the door of the car until one of the men pulled him away and opened it himself. I heard him say, "Where?" and then, "No, it ain't." Then I saw a sudden movement, and some one said, "What was that? Watch him—he threw something away." Two of them caught his arms while the third turned a flashlight on the ground, hunting around with it.

Then Lusby called out: "Miss Louise— Miss Anne! Help me!"

Anne Drayton was there beside me again. "Stay here," she whispered, and ran down the gallery steps.

"You can't do that, Jim!" she said hotly. "He didn't do it! He was in the church—I saw him!"

"Then what's he throwing this away for?"

The man she called Jim held out an oblong leather folder that he'd found with his flashlight.

"Ah never stole it, Miss Anne! She gave it to me to hol'!"

"Yes?" Jim said. "Two hundred-dollar bills and a bunch of traveler's checks. Take him in, you fellows."

He turned back to Anne. I could see the glint of his sheriff's badge as he put the folder in his inside coat pocket.

"Sorry, Miss Anne. We'll have to take him in."

"She gave it to me, to hol' for her!" Lusby said again.

I ran down the steps.

"That's just what she would do!" I cried. "I've seen her do it, lots of times!"

The sheriff looked at me. "Well, we're going to take him in now," he drawled. "We can talk about it in the morning. It won't do him no harm. Nobody's goin' to hurt him."

"Uncle Ed!" Anne cried. She looked past me to where

Judge Drayton was standing quietly on the gallery. "Don't let them take him! You know he didn't do it!"

Judge Drayton came down to the car.

"Go along with them, Lusby," he said. "We'll take care of you in the morning."

He put his hands on Anne's shoulders.

"Oh, how can you let them do that!" she cried. "How can you?"

His hands tightened. "I told you to go to your room, Anne. Go, at once."

She stood there straight and rigid, her burning eyes meeting his without flinching. Then something seemed to happen to her, and she was like a candle on a scorching summer day, as she seemed to droop and bend forward. The next instant she was stumbling across the gallery and through the door. Judge Drayton turned to the sheriff.

"We'll be waiting for you inside. Come, Mrs. Gould."

I went in a little in front of him. I'd have run if I'd dared. I could still feel his eyes, implacable and cold as steel, as he'd bent Anne under them—and I could still feel them when Miss Letty was trying to tell the sheriff what had happened. It was then that I heard her account, or part of it, of Cornelia's telephone conversation, and of her leaving and not coming back.

"And you didn't hear a shot, or anything?" the sheriff asked.

Miss Letty shook her head. "But I had the radio on, and my hearing isn't what it once was."

"You don't know anybody who'd want to kill her?"

Miss Letty shook her head again. The sheriff turned to me. The times I'd said I'd like to strangle Cornelia, after some preposterous performance of hers, flashed into my mind and seemed very stupid now. I shook my head, too.

"Perhaps it was some ghastly mistake," I said.

"Do you mean it was intended for someone else, Mrs. Gould?" Judge Drayton asked quietly.

The implication hung there in a momentary silence.

"Oh, no, of course not," I said. "I didn't mean that."

The sheriff looked around at him. "You weren't here, Judge?"

That embarrassed me still more. I had the feeling that he wouldn't have asked that if it hadn't been for what I'd said.

"Lawrence and I took Anne to the spirituals and left as soon as Mamie was through her part," Judge Drayton said. "We went to the office. We were there when my sister phoned and said Lusby was insisting something must have happened to Mrs. Cartwright. We came back and telephoned around. My son went out to find Anne and Mrs. Gould."

The sheriff nodded.

"What made you think to look in the bayou in the first place?" he asked, with a puzzled frown.

The silence just then was like a creeping paralysis.

"My sister Kate came downstairs," Judge Drayton said, after a moment. "She had gone to bed with one of her headaches. She said she thought she'd heard something in back of the house. She thought it was a shot. That's not uncommon, as you know, but I took a flashlight, and Lusby and I went out to look. That's when I found her."

"What made the boy so sure something had happened to her?"

"I don't know."

"Because Mrs. Cartwright never did unexpected things," I said sharply. "She never let Lusby or her car out of her sight if she could help it."

I felt the skepticism that Mr. Jim Bailey was too polite to utter. He got up.

"Well, I'm sorry about this, Judge." He looked at his watch. "I guess that's Lawrence comin' now."

I could hear a car in the drive. Mr. Bailey and the Judge went out. All I heard was a rather thick "My God!" and then I remembered Lawrence had left before they'd found Cornelia. I looked at Miss Letty. She was like a little snail drawn into its shell, only its feelers showing, sensitive to every sound and motion.

"You'd better go to bed," I said.

"I'd like to wait for Alec."

The clock in the hall struck a single note. I looked at my watch. It was one-thirty.

"Alec can't possibly get here before morning," I said. "Or can he?"

"I don't know, but I want to wait for him," Miss Letty said. "He'd think it was very cruel if somebody didn't sit up and wait."

She shivered convulsively.

"I'll wait up. Somebody ought to wait up with Cornelia. She'll be very lonely and bewildered at first. She won't find any one she knows, not right away."

I looked at her anxiously. If any one else had said it, I'd have thought they were being crazy. But not Miss Letty. I didn't quite like to leave her, and stood there hesitating. Then I heard another car, and in a minute a sharp rap of the knocker on the front door.

"That's Alec," Miss Letty said, starting up. "I know it is. I knew he'd come as quickly as he could."

She turned to me. "Louise—I want you to help me. I want Anne to meet Alec. I'd like her to marry Alec."

Her voice fell to a soft whisper. "Then the plantations won't matter."

For a moment I stood speechless, staring at her. It wasn't that Alec Cartwright wasn't a swell person. It was just that it was so—well, so incredible at that point.

"Go speak to him, Louise," Miss Letty whispered. It was a sort of command that sent me, very bewildered, out into the hall.

Chapter Eleven

STARK TERROR

ALEC CARTWRIGHT and Judge Drayton were standing there.

"I got a plane to bring me up," Alec was saying. He broke off abruptly as he saw me, and took a long stride forward, gripping my hand silently.

"It's awful, Alec," I said. "I'm so sorry."

"What happened? My God, Louise, it doesn't make any sense!"

That was the whole thing, of course. It didn't—not the slightest possible sense. That was what I'd meant when I said it must be a ghastly mistake.

"I thought you'd gone back. The Pilgrimage signs I saw said it ended last Saturday."

"That was the other club," I said. "We just came yesterday."

The sheriff and Lawrence Drayton—rather flushed and unsteady—appeared out of the dining-room. I introduced them.

"If you'll leave us, ma'am," the sheriff said, "I'd like to talk to Mr. Cartwright."

Alec and I looked at each other. He was very good-looking, in a blond, clean-cut way that not even the shocked tension in his face could do very much to diminish. I'd caught Lawrence's instinctive objection to him in his brief handshake and the way he was looking at him now.

"Go to bed, Louise," Alec said. "I'll see you in the morning." He gripped my hand warmly again.

I nodded and went up the stairs. Miss Letty was standing like a dark wraith looking down from the landing. She went on just ahead of me as I came up. As she stopped in the upper hall, I heard Miss Kate Drayton's door close softly.

"Good night, Miss Letty," I said.

"Good night, Louise. We must all be very calm. Remember what I said."

I stood watching her until she went into her room. As I started to open my door, I heard Miss Kate's open quietly. I looked around, just catching one glimpse of her nose and her sharp bright eyes as she closed it again. I opened my door and put my hand out automatically for the switch, and stopped. The light by my bed was already on, and Anne was standing in the shadowy oblong of the window, looking out toward the bayou. Then I realized quickly that it wasn't that; she was looking across the bayou toward Tangiers.

"He must be very uncomfortable over there," she said slowly. "The bathrooms are out on the gallery, and I don't suppose there's ever any hot water."

She closed the screen and came over to the table.

"Have they found out anything?"

I shook my head.

"Alec Cartwright's come. He's her stepson."

"Is he— nice?"

I nodded.

"Then I suppose we'll go to New Orleans tomorrow after all," she said tonelessly. "It's always the way."

"Why don't you just not go?" I asked.

She shrugged.

"I wouldn't have any chance of seeing him if I stayed."

"I don't see how you can help it," I said. "He'll be around till it's settled."

"It would fool them if I *did* marry him, wouldn't it?"

I looked at her in amazement.

"Though I don't suppose he really wants to marry me —not after tonight."

"He can't very well hold this against you," I said.

"But he wanted to know if I wrote that letter. I *did*

insist on some kind of compromise, but my uncle worked it out."

"Look, darling," I said. "Who are you talking about? Alec Cartwright, or—"

"Oh, Lord, no—I meant Steve."

She flushed warmly. "I don't know Alec Cartwright from Adam."

"Well, if it's Steve we're talking about," I said, "I don't think you need worry about not seeing him. He'll manage that."

Her eyes brightened. "Do you think so?"

"Don't be silly," I said. "And you haven't by any chance fallen in love with him, have you?"

She pulled the petals off a rose in the bowl on the table, and looked down at one in her hand.

"You don't fall in love with people you've only seen three times," she said—as if she knew about such things. "But I—I don't know. He's fun. And this afternoon— Well, I don't know. I just can't get him out of my head, Louise. And I know he thinks I'm impossible, and he's just doing it for fun, because he doesn't like Lawrence. I don't think he really cares about the plantations. They aren't worth very much, anyway."

She seemed to be seeking some sort of confirmation, or denial, I wasn't sure which. She was like a child just waking up to an April morning. Death and Cornelia hadn't really touched her.

Then she said, all at once, "If I married him I could go away from here."

"Do you want to go away?"

"Oh, yes!"

It was a heartfelt cry breaking out from somewhere deep inside her.

"Always, really, but not so much as now. I don't know what's happened. Everybody's just as kind as they ever were, but—I feel as if I were on a leash, someway. I can't

see it, but I can feel it. I can go just so far, and then I have
to come back."

She went over to the window and looked out again.

"If you see him tomorrow, will you tell him I didn't
mean what I said—not really."

She stood there for a moment and came back.

"Why do you suppose Lawrence always said he was so
dreadful?"

"For the same reason he told him you were cross-eyed,
I suppose," I said.

"Oh, no—Lawrence didn't do that. That's just part of
the joke," she objected loyally.

"Okay, darling. Now go to bed, will you?"

She laughed. I watched her go happily to the door. She
turned and threw me a kiss. It wasn't for me, really, but
she didn't know it, nor did she know about the new shining light in her eyes. Or that because of it, the carefully
plotted course of murder to come would take a new and
terrible direction.

Oh, well, I thought. I got undressed, went to bed and
turned off my light. I must have dropped off to sleep shortly after that, though it's hard to say when the confused tur-
moil in my mind slipped from disturbed consciousness to
an even more disturbed dream state. Or, for that matter,
when it slipped back again. I know that suddenly I was
awake, staring into the dark, listening intently. I couldn't
imagine what to. There was nothing but silence anywhere
around me. Then, as I lay there straining my ears, I heard
something, like a rat in the plaster behind the head of my
bed—except that it was more methodical than a rat, and
more cautious, some way.

It stopped then, and I waited. It began again. A cold
chill crept along my spine. It was something in Cornelia's
room.

There was a long silence—ages long, it seemed to me—
and then I could hear it again. I sat up in bed, goose-flesh

all over my arms. Some one was in Cornelia's room, going methodically through her things. The sound I heard was the opening and closing of drawers in her dresser and in the big suitcase she carried. I got out of bed, felt around on the rug for my slippers and poked my feet into them. I slipped on my dressing-gown and went quietly to the window.

The moon was still bright, but very high, so that the roof of the gallery secluded all but a tiny narrow strip of silver along the railing. I opened the screen and crept outside. A faint sliver of light showed along the edge of the curtain of Cornelia's window. I edged my way silently toward it, my heart a lump of solid ice sticking in my throat, my body flattened against the brick, the lines of mortar rough and sharp on my back. All I could hear was the thumping of my own pulse.

The crack of light shone steadily, unchanged. I crept on, nearer and nearer, until I could reach out my hand and see the thin slice of yellow across it. I bent forward then and looked.

I could see a huddled figure kneeling on the floor, bending over the bottom drawer of Cornelia's suitcase, lifting her things, feeling through them quickly, laying them in a pile on the floor. I moved back. I didn't have to see the face. The slight, bent shoulders and the hands laying each piece neatly in place were enough. It was Miss Letty.

I edged back against the wall. It was dark as pitch along the gallery. Outside, the world was silver-white. I had got almost to my window when I stopped again, with the same tightening freezing of my heart in my throat. I glanced back. The light was gone, and there was a sound at the screen. But that wasn't what had stopped me—it was something else. It was the crackling rustle of a heavy foot outside, breaking the dry leaves under the magnolia.

I'll never know how I got through the screen as instantly and silently as I did, and across the room to the foot of my bed. There I stopped. I didn't dare get in, for fear of the sound the old springs would make. I stood, gripping the post. I could hear the soft slither of Miss Letty's feet feeling their way cautiously along the gallery floor. My eyes, accustomed to the night now, were fixed on the faint gray oblong of the window, straining to recognize the nuance of a deeper shadow passing across the darkness.

Slowly it emerged. And then I was aware that it was no longer in motion. Miss Letty had stopped at my window and was standing there. At first I couldn't make out— But then I knew. I could hear the faint click of the catch turning. She was coming in. For the first time in my life I knew stark, unmitigated terror.

"Louise?" she whispered.

I didn't know whether to answer her or to scream.

Chapter Twelve

One Footprint Too Many

I WOKE UP, THE SUN cutting brilliantly under the gallery eaves across the bottom of the window screen. I knew at once there was something I had to do, but for a moment I couldn't think what it was. Then I remembered. I got quickly out of bed, went over and unlocked my door. Then I went back and unlocked the screen. If they hadn't been locked, I would have thought I'd dreamed it all.

In the daylight it seemed incredible that I could have stood there by the foot of the bed—with Miss Letty in the window silently opening the screen—motionless, making my breath come evenly, figuring that her eyes, accustomed to the light, wouldn't be able to make out my blurred figure in the dark, not answering her whispered "Louise" on the chance that she was only making sure I wasn't awake. The terror, blind and without reason, when I saw the screen open wider and knew she was coming in, and the almost nauseating sense of relief when I saw her head turn sharply to listen and knew she'd heard the step I'd heard outside on the lawn, because the screen closed quickly and she was gone—swiftly this time, not slowly the way she'd come—all that came back to me.

It came with a kind of unreality that—as I say—I shouldn't have credited if it hadn't been for the locked doors. But now I could see myself, standing there shivering not so much with cold as with sheer nerves, until I was sure she was inside the house, and then creeping over and sliding the catch on the screen. And I'd slipped over and bolted the door before I got back into bed. The eiderdown pulled up over my feet was speaking evidence too of how cold I'd been as I lay there, trying to bring a little order into the chaos of my mind, my eyes glued to the screen until they must have closed from exhaustion.

It didn't seem to be clearer, any of it, this morning—what Miss Letty was doing in Cornelia's room, what Steve was doing again out under the magnolia tree. It all seemed to be nothing but a confusing welter of whats and whys. And the chief and most inexplicable one was "Why Cornelia?" It seemed to me I could have understood almost anybody else. I kept coming back to Lusby, too. They didn't *know* it was the gun in the car that she'd been shot with. Still, the gun was gone, and that was another fact, and it was still another that the only people who knew about its being there were Lusby and Miss Letty and me. Unless, of course, someone had gone through the glove compartment and found it. That was unlikely. People don't normally carry guns in their cars, and people don't rummage through their guests' cars to find out what's in them—supposing it wasn't Lusby or Miss Letty or me who'd done it. I knew I hadn't, and that's all I really did know.

I didn't believe it was Lusby, and I couldn't believe it was Miss Letty. I went back to that again, as I'd done half a hundred times the night before. It was more convincing this morning. Of course there would be a reason for her actions, just as there'd been one for Steve's midnight watch—and just as there'd be one for her telling the sheriff she'd been alone all evening, reading and listening to the radio, until she'd gone to bed, when she'd said to Miss Kate that she could go on destroying the living, but God took care of the dead and would punish Miss Kate as she deserved. In any case—and in the daylight this took on a more convincing authority—Miss Letty just wouldn't kill her best friend.

Or if she had, she'd never have said she wanted Anne to marry Cornelia's son. Except that, of course, Alec wasn't Cornelia's son, just her stepson, and his father, I understood, had liked Miss Letty and she'd liked him.

"Then we won't have to bother about the plantations," she whispered. And Alec would be wealthy. Maybe money was that important—or maybe that was only an afterthought.

While I was dressing I kept going over to the window and looking out. All I could see was the upper part of the magnolia tree, shining lacquered green and velvet-brown in the sunlight. Once I went out on the gallery and looked down at the dry littered leaves underneath it, and then glanced along at the bayou, and turned quickly away. Even then, I knew I had to go down there, if I could, and see for myself where Cornelia had been. It was a kind of magnet that was drawing me. I suppose I didn't like to think of it as just curiosity—but that's a magnetic force even if it drives instead of pulls. Once I looked on beyond the bayou at Tangiers remembering about Anne and how she couldn't get Steve out of her mind.

It was about nine o'clock when I went downstairs. The house was silent as the grave. The front door was shut, and the side shutters closed to keep the sun from fading the carpets and the heavy Victorian draperies, so that the house was dim as well as deserted. I went out on the back gallery. Even the kitchen, connected with the house by a covered passage, was silent. I hesitated for a moment, and then went down the steps and to the right across the grass, and wandered along, trying to be casual about it, toward the bayou.

There was a path through a rose garden, more or less formally laid out, and beyond it were banks of white and pink azalea, all in full glory. No one was in sight anywhere. I came to the end of the roses and onto the grass that sloped down to the bayou, and crossed it, resisting the nagging impulse to keep glancing back at the house.

At the edge of the bayou I stopped and looked along to where the ground was trampled and broken. It was a little to my right, and screened from the side garden, where the magnolia was, by a burst of flowering Japanese peach trees. I went over toward it. It looked as if a band of Indians had had a war dance there, by the slope of the bayou matted with honeysuckle and wild grape, grown with spindly dogwood and redbud trees and other trees and vines that were native and unfamiliar to me. I stopped and looked at the ground caved in where the men had slid down to bring Cornelia up, and turned away for a moment.

She must have fallen against a clump of Spanish dagger growing there. There were brown spots on the pointed leaves, and the moss under it was stained too and broken with heavy feet. I looked back, not at that place but at another that had caught my eye. It was a little to one side, where the vines were pulled and the leaves torn. It wasn't in the direct path that the men had taken—which is why the footprint I saw was still there to be seen, I suppose.

It was the print of a woman's shoe, small with a fairly high heel dug down in the ground, and it was pointed up, not down, as if whoever it was had got down without trouble but had needed the help of the vines to get back up again. I stood looking at it, wondering. Then I looked around to see if there were any more of them. But there weren't—the rest of them had been stamped out by the police.

I heard a footstep behind me, and turned sharply. It was Anne. She looked at me, startled and a little frightened for a moment, and came on quickly.

"I was afraid you were somebody else," she whispered.

She stood behind me looking down the side of the bank in silence.

"It's ghastly, isn't it?" she murmured.

I nodded.

She stood there for a moment. Then I heard her draw her breath in with a sharp sibilant little sound. She was looking at that single footprint under the rope of vines.

She looked away again instantly. "Oughtn't you to go

in and call up your husband and tell him you're all right?"
she said. Her voice was steady but all the color was gone
out of her face.

"I will later," I said. I hadn't even thought of it, as a
matter of fact, and of course he'd be half out of his mind
the minute he saw the morning papers. "Why don't I hang
on to your hand while you pick me that piece of honeysuckle over there?"

She looked at me sharply. Then she said, "All right,"
rather breathlessly. I held her hand while she slid down
and pulled the honeysuckle—and stamped the footprint
out with her heel, pulling down the loose moss-covered
ground. She let go my hand then and glanced with a sort
of reluctant determination toward the Spanish dagger. I
knew she was looking, as I'd looked, for another print of
that tell-tale shoe. Suddenly I saw her move her head forward a little, as if she'd seen something. It wasn't another
footprint, because the expression in her face was surprised
and puzzled, as if she'd seen something she hadn't expected
to see and didn't understand. She looked more intently,
and glanced up at me.

"Is any one coming, Louise?" she asked coolly.

I looked back at the house. As much of the lawn as I
could see through the flowering peach was empty, and no
one was on the upper gallery. I turned back and shook my
head. She put her foot out cautiously and crept down,
keeping her balance with one hand on the trampled earth
bank. Then, just where Cornelia must have been, she
reached her hand gingerly through the spiked stiff leaves
and drew it out.

I saw only a black ribbon in it at first, and then I could
make out something bright and shiny in her hand before
she closed it. She scrambled quickly up the bank again.

· "Let's go," she whispered. "I hear a car. They'll be coming. This way."

She took hold of my arm, and we ran back the way I'd

come until we got to the rose garden.

"Walk," she said. "Toward the oak."

I looked over at the house. Two men were coming. The sheriff was one of them, and I didn't know the other. Anyway, we were out of their sight then, and by the time we got to the marble bench under the oak tree we couldn't even see the part of the bayou they were headed for.

We sat down. Anne held out her hand. She didn't open it at once, and when she did she opened it slowly. The crumpled ribbon fell away, and left Miss Letty's gold locket lying there in the palm of her hand. The emeralds that made the leaves and stem of the little bunch of lilies of the valley sparked in the sun, and so did the rubies that made the bow it was tied with. One of the little pearl flowers was gone.

Anne sat silently, her eyes fixed on it, almost incredulously, it seemed to me. She said, hardly above a whisper,

"How do you suppose that *ever* got there?"

"I think Cornelia Cartwright took it out of your aunt's bag and didn't put it back," I said practically.

"That's funny," she said. "I've never seen it in her things. And how would—"

She stopped abruptly. "Which aunt do you mean?"

"Your Aunt Letty."

She looked at me as if she thought I'd quietly gone out of my mind.

"My Aunt *Letty?*" she gasped.

I could see a whole pattern undergoing an astonished, incredulous transformation.

"Yes," I said, astonished and bewildered myself. "It's hers. She always wears it—or did till we got here. Moreover, she almost cut Cornelia's throat for opening it. That's why Cornelia had it, I imagine. In fact, I know."

She looked at me curiously. "Then you thought that footprint was—"

Her voice trailed out. She looked back at the locket

without saying anything else. I was uncertain and puzzled, not knowing at all what it was she was thinking. She sat there looking at it a long time. Her hand moved, almost as if it moved by itself without her willing it to move, and her fingers touched the little clasp.

I was dying, frankly, to see what was inside it. My tongue was rather like her hand, I suppose, because it said, "I wouldn't, if I were you. She doesn't want anybody to open it."

Her fingers still rested on the clasp.

"I *would* like to know what's in it," she said.

"Have you seen it before—the locket?"

She shook her head. "No. I've never seen it before."

"Then how did you—"

She looked at me and smiled.

"I guess that's part of it," she said. Then she added, without any apparent sense of irrelevance, "You know, my Aunt Kate was a great beauty once."

She looked down at the locket again and closed her hand over it.

"I guess we'd better not open it. Here."

She held it out to me. "If I keep it, I will. I couldn't resist it. You take it and give it back to her. Tell her you found it somewhere."

"Maybe I can't resist either," I said.

I took it from her and held it in my hand. It was oval, about the size of an egg, only flatter, not more than half an inch deep, I should judge. It had the soft gleaming patina of mellowed age. The chasing that formed the frame for the jeweled bouquet had worn down to a delicate shadow. It seemed strange to think that it held in its pale golden stomach something that Miss Letty had gone to God only knew what lengths to preserve, and that if I pressed the tiny catch at the side I'd know instantly what it was. It's not surprising, I suppose, that so many fairy tales, from Pandora through the Arabian Nights, depend

on the box and the last door that must never be opened
when the hero or heroine is left alone with them—or that
curiosity always becomes too strong at last, and sure doom
as surely follows. Cornelia had hardly been a figure in a
fairy tale. Yet her curiosity had driven her to certain be-
trayal of friendship, and how much farther I couldn't say.

I folded the crumpled ribbon, still moist with the dew
caught in the thick blades of the Spanish dagger, around
the little golden and jeweled trinket and put it back in my
pocket. To open it would be like opening a private letter,
or prying loose a friend's locked dresser drawer. And even
apart from the ethics involved, I thought, maybe what was
inside was something that it was better not to know—for
everybody's sake.

Chapter Thirteen

FORGOTTEN PHONE CALL

"I'LL TRUST YOU," Anne said. She smiled, and her face became instantly grave again. "It's funny," she said slowly. "I've decided not to go to New Orleans with Aunt Kate. I don't know what they'll say. And I don't care really. But I'm not going. I guess I'd better tell my uncle."

She looked at me.

"Let me see that again, will you?"

I took the locket out and handed it to her. I'd have given a lot to know what was going on in her mind. She stood there looking at it, her lower lip caught thoughtfully between her white, even teeth. "It's too much for me," she said with a sudden shrug, and handed it back.

We started across the garden. She moved quickly and lightly, with April in her step as well as in her eyes, making me feel like an ancient bumbling clodhopper. She seemed to have forgotten Cornelia and the brown spots beside the Spanish dagger.

A car was coming up the drive. We heard it stop.

"I'll go on," she said. "I don't know how my uncle's going to take it. Don't mention him, will you?"

I knew by now that "him" meant Steve, just as it means God to some people. I dropped behind her. It was the chance I'd been waiting for. The magnolia tree was just across the lawn; I went on casually toward it. The winter leaves, discarded with spring, dried, brown, and crisp, made a carpet around its great trunk. I stooped down and picked one up. It was shiny like gold polished leather. A couple of ants scurried madly across it and underneath. I flicked them off, moving my eyes around the ground at the base of the tree. The leaves were broken and scattered in one place, and I spotted a cigarette butt, stained brown with the dew, and another cigarette half-smoked and crushed as if a foot had pressed it out after it was dropped there.

Then I turned and glanced up at the second story gallery. It was a silly thing to do if I fancied myself as a detective, but it was so automatic that I was hardly aware I'd done it until I looked around and saw Judge Drayton. He was standing a little apart from Alec Cartwright and Lawrence and a man who'd come with them, talking to Anne. Or rather she was talking to him. He was listening with the same apparent concentration with which he'd listened to Millicent and Cora at the candlelight ball, and he was watching me as he'd watched Lawrence then.

I reached down, picked up another leaf and examined it, and went along to join them. I could still feel his gaze following me, and when I came near I looked up.

I said, "Good morning, Judge Drayton."

"Good morning, Mrs. Gould."

He smiled—or his lips did, slightly. His eyes held a flat, incurious quality not unlike a thin, cold breeze through a cracked window onto the back of your neck. I went over to Alec. Lawrence and the other man were moving along toward the bayou.

"Who is that girl?" Alec asked under his breath. "Gosh, she's a beauty."

I nodded to the second and answered the first.

"That's Anne Drayton, the Judge's niece. Haven't you met her?"

He shook his head.

"Married?"

I shook mine. He made an unconscious move to straighten his tie. *Miss Letty doesn't need* my *help,* I thought as he went on looking at her. And well he might. She was radiantly lovely, as casual and natural as the morning, standing there bareheaded, the sun making her hair a fleece of gold, slim and young in her skirt and sweater. Her brown legs were bare, and she had a pair of red socks rolled down around her ankles, and old buckskin moccasin shoes. They were stained a little with dirt from the bayou—but nobody would ever look at her shoes, I thought.

"What about Lusby?" I asked. "Have you got him out?"

Alec Cartwright shook his head. "And what's more, I don't know when we will," he said gravely. "The sheriff's got black spots in front of his eyes. And it does look bad—if you don't know Lusby, or Cornelia."

"What do you mean?" I asked. Perhaps I'd better explain that Alec was fifteen when his father married again, and Cornelia didn't want anyone to think she was his mother, though she was thirty-five then and plenty old enough to have a son that age. That was why she'd had him call her Cornelia instead of Mother or Aunt, as some people do. Alec was about thirty now, I imagine, as Cornelia must have been fifty.

"It gets worse instead of better, too. It seems her watch is gone. I made the mistake of asking about it. Miss Letty told them Cornelia had it in the afternoon, but she hadn't noticed it that night. Also that Cornelia sometimes put it in the ashtray in the seat. Of course, they figure Lusby swiped it. They had the colored gal he took home last night on the carpet, and searched her house."

"But that's ridiculous!" I said warmly.

"I tried to tell them it was. But they knew he was lying."

"What about?"

"He said at first the last time he saw Cornelia was when she told him and the two women he was taking to the church that she'd come later. Now he admits he came right back and saw her again, and that's when she gave him the book of checks."

"You can't think he killed her, Alec," I said.

"No, of course not. I certainly don't. But I'm not running the jail. It's exactly what Cornelia would do. She always thought somebody was trying to get money out of her —you know that. I've seen her when she didn't have ten cents in the house to pay the iceman, because she was afraid to have it around. But, of course, I can't make these dopes believe that. And, of course, Lusby's scared to death. The funny thing about it is I suppose he was really the best friend Cornelia had."

"He certainly put up with enough when she was alive," I said bitterly. "I think it's a beastly shame."

"I'll get a lawyer if he's not out by tomorrow," he said.

I reached in my pocket to get out my handkerchief. My fingers touched the locket. I drew them away as if it had burned them. What if the secret of Cornelia's death lay right there, inside Miss Letty's golden bauble? Would she —I wondered suddenly—let Lusby take the blame?"

"Don't let them take Lusby," she'd said to me.

I put my handkerchief back in my pocket—and I felt, suddenly, the way I did when I found Judge Drayton looking at me. I glanced over at him and Anne. It must have been my own conscience this time, because his back was turned to me—though later I was to suspect more than once that he had eyes there, too. I saw Anne's pleading smile change to satisfaction. She slipped her arm affectionately through his and squeezed it. He patted her hand.

"Don't worry your aunt about it, will you?" he said, as they came toward us.

It struck me then, as it must have struck Cornelia when she was listening to that long controversy between him and his son, that Judge Drayton was really torn between opposing desires—or perhaps between desire and necessity is better. I think he did genuinely love Anne, as strong, hard old men do love some one young and bright and not afraid. That didn't mean he wouldn't sacrifice her. Those two conflicting sides of the man were more plainly written on his face as he and Anne crossed the lawn just then than I ever saw them again—except once, probably.

"This is my niece, Miss Anne Drayton, Mr. Cartwright," he said gravely.

Anne held out her hand.

"I'm so sorry," she said simply.

"Thank you, Miss Anne," Alec said. "You've all been very kind."

It was natural for Steve Heywood to pop into my mind just then, I suppose because Alec held her hand longer than was necessary or even polite. I saw Judge Drayton's guarded inquisitorial face become a little closer guarded, all of a sudden, as if he sensed an unnecessary complication in a situation already too complicated for his liking—one that he definitely didn't like, and that I easily guessed, furthermore, he had no intention of allowing.

"I'm going in and phone to my husband, Judge Drayton, if you don't mind," I said.

It seemed to me it might be awfully simple for Alec Cartwright just to step in and substitute his image for Steve's, and divert a waking emotion that couldn't be very firmly grounded as yet. The idea that I was being disloyal to both Miss Letty and Alec, for some one I scarcely knew, occurred to me as I started for the house, but it didn't impress me very much. As I reached the gallery I heard Anne call. She was coming after me. One look at her face told me something had happened in the brief time since I'd walked away from them. She took my arm.

"You've got to call him," she whispered. "They're going to arrest him."

"Arrest him!" I gasped. "What for?"

"I don't know. My uncle just said if they got him they'd probably let Lusby go. Hurry! We've got to warn him. Oh, dear, I knew something—"

She didn't go on. She gave the operator a number and then handed the phone to me. I shook my head.

"Go on," I said. "I'll stand guard."

"Hello," she said quickly. "Tangiers? Mr. Steven Heywood, please."

I saw the flush that asking for him brought into her cheeks fade out slowly until her face was as colorless as the bowl of azaleas on the desk behind her. She put the phone down unsteadily.

"He's gone," she said. "He left early this morning. And —he took his things with him. He—he's not coming back any more."

She went blindly over to the window and stood with her back to me, her hands hanging limply down at her sides. She wasn't crying. She was too stunned to cry, and too proud, I suppose. I could see as plainly as if she'd told me that she'd been building up their next meeting—what she'd say to him and what he'd probably say back—and that the brief fear of his being arrested was only an interlude in all that. It was her pride and her vanity as much as it was her heart that was crushed.

"I guess he—he had enough of his silly joke," she said without turning her head.

She fished an envelope out of her pocket and tore it up. "I'm glad I didn't send that."

She turned, picked a match off the desk, lighted it, tossed the burning paper into the fireplace and watched it curl into black carbon ribbons. Then she looked at me and smiled, not very convincingly.

"Well, that's that." She brushed her hands lightly together, dismissing the whole thing. "Let's you and me go to a movie tonight, shall we? It would be all right, wouldn't it?"

Cornelia's shadow was in the room again.

"I should think so," I said. Anything to get Steve out of her mind, I thought. Somehow I could see him waking up in his room at Tangiers (the one with the tin cradle bath in it, no doubt), looking at the ceiling and suddenly saying, "Oh, the hell with it—what's the use? She's a nice kid, let her have the plantations," and just clearing out, maybe not entirely without the idea that if he'd stayed longer it mightn't be so easy to go as he planned it to be. She hadn't given him any reason to think she'd want it otherwise, heaven knows.

"I don't really *care*, Louise," she said abruptly. "I wouldn't want you to think that."

"Oh, dear, no—of course not," I said.

"Because, after all, I only saw him three times. It would be silly to—to—"

"Very," I agreed. *If she doesn't stop, I'm going to weep,* I thought. First love can hurt so much worse than the mumps.

She fished her lipstick out of her pocket and stood on tiptoes to look in the mildewed mirror over the mantel, glancing toward the door. They were coming into the house, heavy shoes clattering on the parquet floor. The sheriff, Mr. Jim Bailey, was saying, "Don't worry, he won't get far. The state patrol'll pick him up. He hasn't crossed the river—I've already checked up on that."

Anne turned to me, and stood there staring. "Louise! What's the matter!"

"Nothing," I said. But there was. It had just flashed into my mind. I'd forgotten all about it until that minute. It had happened at the hotel, before Steve took me over and left me at the colored church.

"It's twenty to eight," I'd said. "We'd better push off. I'm meeting the Draytons."

We'd been talking about Cornelia and about his Aunt Selina, and how women who controlled large wealth supported foreign missions and dog and cat hospitals first and children's aid third.

"Pay the check, will you?" he asked. "I've got to make a phone call. Haven't got two nickels, have you?"

He put down a five-dollar bill and a dime.

"Going to call up your girl?" I asked sardonically.

"Yeah. What's her number?"

"Just ask for Antigua," I said.

And that had been a quarter of eight—and Cornelia had answered the phone.

Chapter Fourteen

DEAD WOMAN'S JEWELS

"IT'S FUNNY HE'D SKIP out that way," Alec Cartwright was saying in the hall.

"What *is* it, Louise?"

"It's nothing, Anne," I repeated. "I just feel a little dizzy. It's the sun, maybe."

"Mrs. Gould seems to know him," Judge Drayton was saying. "You might ask her."

And that was the trouble. I didn't know him. I'd met him at a service station on the Natchez Trace. I didn't know him at all. And Anne must have understood. She took hold of my hand.

"This way. We can go up the gallery steps."

She pushed open the window screen and we slipped out and up the wooden stairs to the second gallery and into the hall. Miss Letty, just starting down the stairs, looked at us with surprise.

"Anne dear," she said then, "I want you to come down with me and meet Alec Cartwright."

You couldn't tell about Miss Letty's face. It always looked troubled, but I thought it looked more so than usual at the lack of enthusiasm in Anne's voice. "I've met him."

"Then come down with me and talk to him," Miss Letty said. She held out her hand. "This is all so difficult for him —he needs somebody to talk to."

As Anne glanced at me I nodded. I thought Miss Letty was making a mistake, trying to cram him down her throat this way, but that wasn't my affair. After all, Alec was a lot better than Lawrence.

"Okay," Anne said.

"Be nice to him for my sake, won't you, Anne?"

They went down the stairs together, and I went on to my room and stood there by the window looking across the garden toward Tangiers. It wasn't as far away as it had seemed the first night I'd looked at it. Now that I was orientated I realized that probably two city blocks lay between the entrance of Antigua and the gate into Tangiers. The Heywood house would be closer to the bayou, because it wasn't as imposingly extensive as Antigua. It was also dingier and more vine-covered, and it needed paint. Through the screen of foliage I could see an expanse of lawn and a tangled garden. It was a silent kind of place, and an occasional yapping dog seemed to intensify its silence rather than give it life. It seemed to me that if Cornelia had been murdered there, it wouldn't have been so surprising and incongruous as it was that she should have been murdered here at Antigua. Except for Miss Kate Drayton, who as far as I could make out never seemed to leave her room, much less the house, Antigua was as modern and normal as Cornelia's own elaborate menage at home.

As I was looking across the bayou I saw someone come out on the second gallery. It was a woman. She stood there a long time, looking toward Antigua. I wondered what she was thinking about. What happened, I wondered too, between that house and this one? Not even in the South would two families so close together, with young people—for even Judge Drayton and Miss Kate had been young once, and so had the woman on the gallery across the bayou—have carried on a feud over a romance three-quarters of a century old, however bloody its outcome had been.

There must be something else, I thought, to make Judge Drayton say all Heywoods were skunks. And it was odd how little I knew about any of them. Mr. Minot Heywood, for example. How had he died, and when? Nobody had said. And the other Drayton—Anne's father. Why had he left home and gone East when he was young? I put my hand in my pocket suddenly. Miss Letty's locket was still there. I took it out and looked at it. Maybe the answer to all of it was what was inside, and was what Miss Letty had turned into a sudden jungle-cat to keep Cornelia from knowing.

My reason told me I didn't want to know what was in that locket—and another part of me stronger than reason kept telling me I really ought to know—if I knew, perhaps I could help. But I knew too that that wouldn't be why I opened it. I put it back quickly. I had to find Miss Letty at once, and give it to her before I was sorry.

I put on my hat and gloves and started downstairs. Halfway down I heard a bright, flat voice.

"Of course I know Mr. Cartwright. I never forget a face —I've trained myself. People are always so surprised. I recognized you the minute I first saw you. You're so like poor dear Cornelia. I wanted you to know how deeply I sympathize with you. It's a *great* loss. I've written a memorial to read to our chapter. I want you to let me know if there's anything I can do."

They were in the front parlor. I heard Alec murmur something polite about how kind she was. If I went *quietly*, I thought—but I was wrong. Anne spotted me.

"Oh, Louise, come in! You know Mrs.— I'm sorry, I—"

"Mrs. Storm—Philander Storm."

"How do you do?" I said. I looked around for Cora, but she wasn't there.

"My dear, I can't tell you how upset I am. Cornelia was a *great* woman. A great loss."

She flowed on and on. Poor Alec mopped his forehead surreptitiously. I wondered if it occurred to him how much like Cornelia she was. She looked like her, and went on and on like her. It was as if it were no longer Cornelia's shadow in the house but herself. Anne looked at me helplessly.

"I wonder if you wouldn't like to see Antigua, Mrs. Storm," she put in. "We aren't open for the Pilgrimage, but—"

I doubt if there was much Mrs. Philander Storm hadn't already seen. Her eyes had been darting around like dragonflies while she was talking. I thought for an instant it was that she'd come for, really—but I was wrong.

"I'd love it, my dear. It's a beautiful house—simply enchanting. You're so lucky. Just think of being born here."

"I wasn't," Anne said. "I was born in Atlanta, Georgia."

"Oh, then you must have loved *Gone with the Wind*. But you were born here, weren't you?"

She smiled brightly at poor little Miss Letty, and then stopped.

"This is my other aunt, Miss Drayton," Anne said quickly. "This is Mrs. Storm, Aunt Kate. An old friend of Mrs. Cartwright's."

"How do you do, Miss Drayton?"

Millicent was off again. And then I saw her eyes fixed on a small Bennington jug on the candle stand beside the piano. She darted at it and picked it up.

"Wedgewood, isn't it? I love Wedgewood!"

Miss Kate Drayton, her hands folded in front of her, curiously small and elegant and white compared with her tall angularity, moved forward and took it politely out of her hand.

"It is Bennington ware," she said. "It belonged to my grandmother."

"Oh, of course. But it is lovely."

Mrs. Storm turned quickly. "Mr. Cartwright, I hope you won't think I'm being a ghoul, but you know how collectors are. I'm a collector, and my husband says I'm absolutely without shame, but that's not true. I know you'll understand, because I was deeply devoted to your dear mother."

We waited.

"Your mother was showing me a piece of jewelry she had. It isn't of any great value, and it's not the sort of thing a young man would want, or appreciate for his wife, unless she happened to be particularly interested. So I'd like to buy it from you."

"If you mean the diamond wrist watch, Mrs. Storm, it's disappeared," Alec said stiffly.

"Oh, dear, no," Mrs. Storm laughed. "It was just a battered old locket. I don't suppose it was gold really, probably silver washed with gold."

I didn't look at Miss Letty. I didn't have to. I could feel her, the way some people can feel a cat walk into a room.

"It has a spray of imitation emerald and pearl lilies of the valley on it, tied with a garnet bowknot, and was quite—"

There was a violent crash behind me. I flashed around. Miss Kate Drayton was staring at her, her face the color of an old muslin coffee-strainer. The Bennington jug was in a thousand pieces on the floor at her feet.

It was I who got Mrs. J. Philander Storm out of the house. I didn't know how long the Drayton good breeding could continue, after Miss Kate's appalling lapse from it, even after Anne had managed to get her out of the room. I never looked at Miss Letty—I didn't dare. I just said, "Don't you think we'd better go, Mrs. Storm?" and she was so astonished she came without a murmur.

Until we got in her taxi, that is. "Well, what on earth do you suppose—"

"I don't know," I said. "I guess she was shocked at your wanting to buy a dead woman's jewelry. Would you mind dropping me at the next corner?"

"You don't suppose she dropped it in the ditch there, do you?" Mrs. Storm asked, as I got out.

"Probably," I agreed ironically.

Chapter Fifteen

HIGH-PITCHED SCREAM

ALL THAT AFTERNOON Miss Letty's bauble was like a piece of radium in my jacket pocket. If I'd seen an open man-hole with nobody looking, I'd have dropped it in just to be rid of it. My mind was like a blindfolded horse I once saw in France, going round and round and round on a treadmill. Each new solution of the problem that I came to was more fantastic and improbable than the one I'd given up before it, and none of them, I didn't doubt, was less than a hundred miles from the truth.

Still, I resisted opening it, grimly but honestly, until late that afternoon. I'd gone down to the river, because I didn't want to go back to the house. I didn't want to go on with the Pilgrimage either, because one of the hostesses or a newspaper man might recognize me, and it was bad enough as it was. I sat on a bench on the bluff looking across the lazy, unlovely Father of Waters toward the flat Louisiana shore. I was hardly aware that I'd taken the locket out of my pocket and was holding it in my hand. And suddenly the impulse was overwhelming, and my fingers were on the tiny snap. It stuck—thank heavens—for just the fraction of an instant—or maybe my fingers were shaking, because a car had stopped behind me and I heard Mrs. Philander Storm.

"Your club did all this landscaping?" she was saying. "It's quite nice, for a small place like Natchez. But as I was saying, I think she must have run on to something, and that's why they killed her. Well, my dear, I wouldn't have be—"

The car moved on. I sat there quietly. My hands were cold as ice. "I don't want to die," I whispered to the white azaleas on the bank of the Mississippi. I put the locket away. It was no longer a lovely old-fashioned thing holding a woman's secret. It was a sinister thing that had lain all night in the blood-tipped Spanish dagger, a thing of danger and jealousy and fear.

It was five o'clock when I got back to Antigua. Alec and Lawrence and Anne were sitting out on the back gallery, away from the curious eyes that kept peering up from the closed gates. The older Draytons were upstairs. I started out to join them when the telephone rang in the library.

"Shall I answer it?" I said, still in the doorway. I saw the quick hope that flashed in Anne's eyes, and died instantly, remembering.

"Sure," Lawrence said. "And if it's another reporter tell him to go to hell."

I went back and picked up the phone. My heart jumped.

"Oh, Lord!" I said. "Where *are* you?"

"One is in town, a fugitive from justice," Steve Heywood's voice said cheerfully. He went on with a more sardonic tone. "I haven't decided whether to give myself up yet or not. I want to see you first. What about meeting me at that dump where we had the hot dogs?"

A funny little malease about the size of a fruit worm did a half-turn in my heart. I hesitated.

"At about seven-thirty," he said. "I'll be disguised as a Coldstream Guard with a bearskin toupee."

"All right," I said.

"And look, Louise. Find out where they've sent her, will you? She's in my bloodstream—I've got to see her again before they hang me."

I stared blankly into the wall. I'd forgotten that. He thought she'd gone away.

"Of course," I gasped. "All right. I will. Seven-thirty. Good-by."

I hung up and stood there for a moment. You'd have thought it was I that was in love with him. I started to whistle happily. Then suddenly, halfway back to the porch, I remembered—or maybe by some process of delayed audition I was just hearing—the ominous, almost silent click of another telephone being put cautiously and stealthily back into place before I'd hung up.

Oh, dear, I thought. I glanced up the stairs. I hadn't thought of that.

"Who was it, Louise?" Lawrence called.

"Nobody," I said casually, coming out on the gallery. At least I thought I was being casual. Maybe I wasn't, for instantly Anne's eyes were shining like a couple of tropical stars. She looked down quickly, but it was something she couldn't hide. If Lawrence had ever been particularly aware of her he must have seen it, but as he wasn't he just went on talking. Alec, I think, thought any change was for him, because she gave him a smile when he retrieved a magazine she dropped that would have blinded the Great Sun. Though that's absurd, because the Natchez Indians didn't like the white people very much after they knew them better.

"What time are we going to the movie, Louise?" she asked suddenly. "I hope you don't mind our going," she said to Alec.

"Of course not. I'd like to go along, but I don't suppose—"

"Not in Natchez. They'd think you did it yourself," Lawrence said. "I guess I'll have to go with them. What's the picture?"

Anne swallowed. She was as transparent as a soap bubble.

"I thought you were going on the fox hunt?"

She managed to sound remarkably casual. I shook my head at her. I was desperately afraid she'd say too much.

"Father thought it wouldn't look right."

The subject dropped for a moment, but I was on pins and needles. I didn't know how I was going to let Steve know. And there was still that ominous click of the other phone to be reckoned with. Anne sat with a fixed unnatural smile on her face that showed how little used to deception of any kind she was.

"We got Lusby out on bail, Louise," Alec said.

"That's fine," I said.

"I hope he doesn't skip it," Lawrence remarked skeptically. "They haven't got Heywood yet, I understand."

Anne flushed, but she held her tongue, and so did I. Judge Drayton's appearance just then didn't help me any, but it was a relief to her.

"Do you think it would be all right if we went to the movie, Uncle Ed?" she asked.

He shook his head. "No, I think you'd better stay at home tonight, Anne," he said quietly—so that I knew instantly what I'd already known perfectly well.

"We could slip in to the early show, Father," Lawrence said. "Alec understands we don't mean any disrespect to his mother."

I felt the subtle change in the Judge's attitude as acutely as I'd have felt it if some one had taken a thick screen from in front of a fire.

"In that case, I think it would be all right. I don't like to have two young women out at night by themselves."

He's going to tell the sheriff, I thought. *He's probably done it already. Then Steve will think I gave him away.*

"Be back early," Judge Drayton said.

We set out in Anne's car. She was amazingly cool, and I soon realized that she knew Lawrence a lot better than I did. She slowed down when we got to Main Street and stopped the car. "Look," she said. "There's Mike."

"Hi, boy," Lawrence called. He got out and went over to a group of men, some in high leather boots and rough clothes, gathered on the corner. In a minute he came back. "Look, why don't we all go out? You don't want to go to a movie. It's a rotten picture anyway."

Anne shook her head.

"You go on if you want to. Nobody'll know the difference."

Lawrence hesitated. "If I don't stay very long, I could meet you at the coffee shop."

I suppose I ought to explain that they hunt foxes at night with hounds view-hallooing across the bayous, and the spectators follow in cars along the road, and drink out of bottles unless somebody has brought a cup along, and sometimes the fox crosses the road and sometimes a hound gets bored and comes back and joins the spectators. Lawrence was going as a spectator.

"Good-by," Anne called cheerfully. "Now where is he?" she demanded. "And what did he say?"

"He thought you'd gone to New Orleans," I said. "And he wanted your address. There was some nonsense about your being in his bloodstream. He's at that service-station inn on the road where we went to the ball the first night."

He was there, all right, at fifteen minutes past seven, slumped down behind the wheel of his open car. And that wasn't all. Anne touched my arm. Leaning against a gas pump was one of the men the sheriff had with him in the morning. What he was waiting for I didn't know until he took out his watch and looked at it. He went inside.

"Quick," Anne said.

She drove her car in beside Steve's. He looked up. For a minute he didn't believe he was seeing her. Then he grinned.

"Hullo," he said.

They both looked at me. "I'm going to a movie," I said.

"Take my car—I'll go with Steve," Anne said. "And we'd better hurry."

She slipped out, and in beside him. I watched them go down the road. It wasn't a minute too soon. The deputy sheriff came out just then, looked at his watch again and stared at a car coming in. It was Cornelia's limousine with

Lusby at the wheel and Alec in the back. Miss Letty was with him, talking earnestly. I pulled the sun screen around to shade my face, finished my sandwich and coffee and went on to the movie. My only qualm was that they might not get back by ten o'clock—not to mention what Judge Drayton was going to say if and when he found out about them. I didn't, as a matter of fact, care very much. I was just determined that Anne Drayton wasn't going to marry her cousin Lawrence—and I didn't think she had a chance in a thousand to marry Alec, in spite of Miss Letty. Cornelia's account of the conversation between Lawrence and his father was altogether too vivid in my mind.

At ten o'clock I came back to the service station. The electric victrola was blaring out horribly, and the place was packed with cars. Steve and Anne were nowhere in sight. I ordered a hamburger and a cup of coffee and waited. After a while I ordered another hamburger and coffee and waited again. At a quarter to eleven I saw the sheriff and the man who'd been there earlier drive up, look around and order a hot dog. At least *they* hadn't found them, I thought. At eleven o'clock they looked around again and left.

I didn't know what to do. I didn't know whether to go to the coffee shop and see if Lawrence was there, or what. The cars were leaving one by one, and a few trucks began to pull in. Still I waited, the minutes dragging unbelievably and a thousand ghastly doubts creeping suddenly around inside me—an accident on the road and both of them dead, their car parked on a lonely roadside and a maniac attacking them—all the terrible things that can and do happen to people. Finally at half past eleven I couldn't stand it any longer. I paid my bill, switched on the ignition, and backed out into the road.

There was no use trying to find them, along the moonlit chasms of those deep-cut roads, and I was almost frantic. If anything had happened to them, how could I ever explain? And then came the most horrible doubt of all, and it had really been there all the time, made up from that telephone call of the night before, the momentary alarm when Steve had asked me to meet him, Cornelia's fears along the road coming to Natchez. It sat beside me in the car like those awful pictures of Death Beside the Drunken Driver.

I pressed my foot on the accelerator and gripped the wheel to keep the light car on the road. It was only a few minutes later that I suddenly realized I'd missed the turn into Albemarle Street and gone on without knowing it, and that I was lost and going in the wrong direction, heavens knew where. The houses I'd passed along the street were dark. I came at last to one that was dimly lighted. *I can ask there,* I thought, and went on up to it.

At the end of the road I came to a dead stop. I was at Tangiers. Steve's car was there in the yard under an oak. I jumped out and tugged at the broad wooden gate, trying to open it. And then suddenly my blood froze to a motionless, burning stream of ice. A high-pitched, incredibly piercing scream, of a woman's voice, split the night, shattering the moonlit silence as if into a million glancing sparks. It broke off, abruptly, terribly, half-uttered, echoing and breaking off again—and then it was gone, and all there was was empty, deathly silence.

I stood there for an instant, motionless with fright, and then tugged furiously at the gate. It wouldn't move. I climbed over the bars and ran desperately past the house and down the garden toward the bayou. There was still no sound, not even a dog rushing out to bark as I broke through the tangled flower bed trying to find a path. Then behind me I heard a door opening. I didn't look back; I just ran on, almost beside myself with dread. Why had I let her go? Why had I been so utterly blind as not to understand?

Across the dark street of the bayou I could see Antigua,

all its lights spring up, and I could see the flash of darting lights in the garden there and hear people shouting and running toward me. Then I was through the screen of trees at the end of the path and running across the strip of uneven ground to the edge of the bayou. I heard another shout, closer:

"This way! Over here!"

It was Steve Heywood. I could see him clearly in the brilliant white moonlight. He was kneeling on the ground. People were crashing up out of the bayou from the other side.

"Hurry!" he shouted. "Hurry!"

His back was toward me, and all I could see was a dark figure lying in front of him on the ground. A nauseating wave caught me. I swayed for a moment and went on again, just as Alec Cartwright and Lawrence cleared the bayou and got up to him. Alec's flashlight fell on the figure lying there.

"My God!" he said.

Lawrence grabbed my arm and steadied me as my knees just turned to water. It wasn't Anne. That was all I knew, and for one terrible instant all I cared. It wasn't Anne.

"They went down that way," Steve said curtly. He pointed to the far end of the bayou just as Judge Drayton came heavily up out of it, through the broken track Alec and Lawrence had made. His face looked gray in the moonlight, and he clutched at his coat front, reeling a little just as I had done, caught himself and came on.

"It's that woman—what was her name?" Lawrence said hoarsely.

"Storm. Her name was Storm," Steve said.

"Mrs. J. Philander Storm. Cornelia called her Millicent."

It was I saying that. I was aware of my voice sounding lost, like a dead leaf falling.

Chapter Sixteen

MURDER WITHOUT MOTIVE

FOR AN INSTANT we all stood there motionless. I knew that each of us—except Steve—had thought it was somebody else, not Millicent Storm. But we couldn't *all* have thought it was Anne, I said to myself stupidly.

Steve straightened up. "She's dead," he said. "She was lying on her face here. I heard her scream. That must be hers over there."

He pointed to a huge flashlight lying on the grass. Alec Cartwright swung his flash on it. It had a thin smear of blood on it, glistening, alive.

"You stay here with Louise, Judge Drayton," Steve said curtly. "They can't have got very far. Come on, you two. We'll close in along this damn ditch."

They started off. Judge Drayton knelt down and put his handkerchief over Millicent Storm's face. He stood there for a moment with his head bowed, then raised it abruptly. The three men stopped short in their tracks. I could hear the sound of breaking undergrowth from the bayou, and waited, my heart like something bitter and undigested in the pit of my stomach, too numb for fear, just waiting to see. Then out of the dense shadows a figure emerged. I heard Judge Drayton's swift intake of breath.

"Kate!" he said, his voice just part of that breath.

Miss Drayton scrambled up onto firm ground. "I was coming—I lost my way," she gasped.

There was a sharp silence. The three men had stopped and were standing motionless, watching her come unsteadily toward us.

"Who is it?" she said. "What's happened? Don't just stand there."

"It's Mrs. Storm. She has been killed," Judge Drayton said evenly.

"Who on earth is Mrs. Storm?"

"The lady who was at the house this morning, Kate."

"Oh." Miss Kate stood there. "The woman who—"

"Yes," Judge Drayton said.

"I do declare," Miss Kate said.

It seemed extraordinary that she should take it so calmly when what would seem a trivial thing compared with it had shocked a valuable Bennington jug out of her hands to shatter on the floor. But perhaps it was just the words that were inadequate, I thought. I was terribly shocked, myself, and yet if I'd said the things racing through my mind they would have seemed just as unaffected by the central fact of Millicent Storm's dead body.

I was wondering where Anne was, first, and what Steve had been doing down there. He certainly hadn't come from the house, yet he was there minutes before Lawrence and Alec broke through the tangle of the bayou. He must have thought, of course, that she was still alive, or he wouldn't have been shouting, "Hurry!" the way he was. I wondered, too, where Miss Letty was, and how it happened that Alec was there. If he'd brought her back to Antigua and hadn't yet gone back to his hotel, it was odd she hadn't come along. If Miss Kate could make it, she certainly could. And why hadn't Lusby come? I even wondered, quite irrelevantly, if Judge Drayton had a bad heart, from the way he'd clutched his coat front as he came up the bank.

And—perhaps above all—why whoever it was I'd heard open the door in Tangiers as I ran down the path hadn't come—or were they going in, not coming out at all? And why hadn't the dogs barked? Then I wondered what anybody would do if he got down into the bayou. Where did it go to? Or would whoever had struck down Millicent Storm have needed to go down. I stopped there. I didn't want to think of that.

Miss Kate was saying tartly, "Has any one thought of calling the police? Or are we going to stand here doing nothing?"

Lawrence started off. "I'll telephone."

"You'd better go to Tangiers, it's closer," Steve said.

Judge Drayton spoke sharply. "Go to Antigua, Lawrence."

"And if many more of you go through, there won't be anything left for the police," Steve remarked.

Lawrence went on. I could see his light flashing through the tangled greenery, and I heard him swear once when he slipped.

"What could she have been doing down here, in the first place?" Miss Kate said. "It seems very peculiar to me."

It was, very, of course, I thought at first. Then I had a sick feeling that it was all my fault. Mine and the gold locket that I still had wrapped in my handkerchief in my pocket—afraid to put it anywhere else until I could give it to Miss Letty, for fear she'd go through my things, too, and find it, and—I didn't go any further with that either. If I hadn't said, "Probably," when Mrs. Storm asked if I didn't think Cornelia had dropped the locket in the bayou, she wouldn't have been here. And yet she hadn't looked like a brave woman to me. I couldn't imagine her trekking down here at night. Even if it was as light as day on the open moonlit lawns, it was mostly black as pitch in the bayou. There might be snakes, too, though I understood they didn't come out until later when it was warm. Still, there wasn't any other reason I could imagine, unless she'd come to meet someone. But whom, or why?

"I think I'll go back to the house, Brother," Miss Kate said. "Will you come, Mrs. Gould?"

"I'll stay, I think," I said.

"Suit yourself," she answered. "Will you kindly help me through the bayou, Mr. Cartwright?"

"I'm beginning to think you people don't want the tracks left," Steve remarked.

"Perhaps we don't think it necessary, Mr. Heywood," Judge Drayton said.

They faced each other, cool and grim.

"May I ask what the hell you mean by that, sir?"

"I think we can let the sheriff decide it," Judge Drayton returned.

I put my hand on Steve's arm. "Shut up," I said softly.

Alec Cartwright came over and stood beside me. It was sort of the three "outsiders" together. Steve shrugged, took out a pack of cigarettes, and lighted one. And that sent a chilly wave down my spine. I hadn't yet had time to ask what he'd been doing there under the magnolia tree across the bayou.

He turned to Alec. "I'm sorry about your mother. I understand they're hunting me in connection with it. I left this morning because I had business to see to. I was out having a look at a couple of plantations a cousin of my father's left in his will."

He was talking to Alec but looking at Judge Drayton. It's hard to describe a sudden stiffening of a human body without making it sound melodramatic. It wasn't exactly a stiffening, either, in Judge Drayton. It was just as if he'd contracted all over, or become awfully still, as a lizard does when he thinks danger is too close to get away from.

"I believe my niece withdrew her very liberal proposal, Heywood," he said evenly.

"I think your niece really thought it was liberal, Judge Drayton," said Steve. He dropped his cigarette on the ground and put his foot on it. That bothered me too. "I don't for a moment believe she had any idea there was presumed to be oil on the three plantations she was keeping, and none on the two she offered me."

"My dear sir," Judge Drayton said. He laughed as if it were not quite mildly amusing. "You've been talking to some of the local Wallingfords."

"No," Steve said. "I just looked around a bit. Whoever took the red and yellow ribbons off the fences at Araby and Tivoli and Avon dropped a couple. He also left some threads where he ripped them off. I understand there's a little skulduggery about the leases, too."

"The leases weren't renewed because the oil companies considered they were barking up the wrong tree," Judge Drayton said. "However, since it doesn't concern you personally I shall not discuss it further."

"I think it does, you know," Steve said coolly. "We can discuss it later."

It looked to me for a moment as if the rigid control Judge Drayton had over the temper that went with the Drayton eyes was going to snap. He took a long breath. "The discussion is ended at this point, Mr. Heywood."

"If I persuade your niece to marry me, I believe it *is* ended, Judge Drayton. And that is what I hope to do, sir."

I saw Alec look at him blankly. Even at such a time, and standing there where I was, I had an almost irresistible desire to laugh. I didn't really know what he thought about Anne, but certainly no one had told him about Steve. Or even Lawrence, probably, I thought.

I heard a car come up and the sound of feet running toward us.

"That is—impossible, Mr. Heywood. If you'll come to my office tomorrow, I will tell you why. If you are able to come," he added quietly.

"Fortunately, I'm white," Steve said imperturbably. "I'll be there."

The men were crashing down the bayou and up our side—Jim Bailey, his deputy, and Lawrence. Alec drew me a little to one side.

"What's all this about?" he whispered.

"Steve wants to marry Anne and they don't want him to," I answered. "They want her to marry Lawrence."

"That pipsqueak?"

"Sssh," I said. "It's just to keep the oil wells in the family, I gather."

"That must have been what Cornelia meant," he returned. "She telegraphed me." He gripped my arm sharply. "Listen, for God's sake."

" . . . saw him," Lawrence Drayton was saying. He was pointing to Steve standing a little off from them. The rest were in a kind of semicircle, with the body of Millicent Storm there on the ground between them.

"I was coming in the back way so as not to disturb the family. He was sneaking down the garden path, coming this way. I thought what the hell, but I didn't see any use trying to stop him."

"You knew we wanted him," Jim Bailey said.

"I was going in to phone you. I knew you'd find him at Tangiers. I didn't know whether he still had a gun on him. Anyway, I'm not the sheriff."

"Go on," Bailey said shortly.

"I got about halfway up the stairs to the second gallery when I heard the scream. I ran down to the library and got this."

He took a small automatic revolver out of his pocket, showed it and slipped it back.

"Then I ran over here, Cartwright there caught up with me and we got here together. It couldn't have been more than three minutes. He was kneeling down there by her, yelling, 'Hurry up,' and pointing down that way, saying somebody had run down through the bayou."

He glared angrily around the grim-faced circle. Steve looked calmly at him, apparently unconscious of the five pairs of eyes fixed steadily on him. I glanced quickly at Judge Drayton. He looked like an El Greco of the Inquisition, brilliant-eyed, his face gray and obsidian, with a quality of mercilessness that if it had had triumph in it would have been less awful than it was. It hadn't. No one would have guessed his quiet "If you are able" was being settled so quickly the way he wished it.

"I'd like to say something, if I may," Steve observed coolly.

"You'll have plenty of time," somebody put in, with a kind of grim humor.

"I'd like to say it now. You're the sheriff, aren't you?"

"Go ahead," Jim Bailey said.

"I was coming down the garden path across there. I wasn't sneaking, because I hadn't been to the fox hunt and I didn't have to sneak in the back way."

"What were you doing then?" Lawrence said.

"That's my business. I got to the edge of the bayou and was trying to find the way down when I heard the scream. I haven't got a gun. I don't own one. Then I dashed down the back through the vines and up here. I heard somebody breaking through the undergrowth but I thought I saw her move, and I thought maybe I could do something for her. I didn't have a light, and I didn't see hers right away. When I did, she seemed to move again, so I tried to work on her."

"Explaining why your fingerprints'll be on her flash, I suppose," Lawrence said.

"You go to hell. I'm telling what happened."

"What were you doing at Antigua?" Bailey asked.

"I'm sorry I can't tell you."

"When did you come back to Natchez, Heywood—or is Maxwell the name?"

"The name's Heywood, and I didn't come back, because I never left. I was out in the country looking at Minot Heywood's plantations—Araby, Tivoli, and Avon. I got back about a quarter to five."

"You made an appointment with this lady for seven-thirty. What for?"

"I wanted to see her."

"Did you know we were looking for you?"

"Yes. Miss Rose Heywood told me."

"Why didn't you give yourself up?"

"I was going to come and see you as soon as I got around to it," Steve said calmly. "If it hadn't been for Miss Rose's being so upset about it I'd have thought it was too damned cockeyed to be true. I never spoke to Mrs. Cartwright but once in my life, and that was because a friend of mine pulled a fast one on me at Melrose. I had to listen to her explain the parlors."

"Then how did she happen to know you as Maxwell?"

"That's my aunt's name. Mrs. Cartwright knew her and called me by her name. That's all."

"Then who is this woman?"

"Her name's Storm."

"You ever seen her before?"

"Yes. She was staying at Tangiers. She came the day I did. I've said good morning to her, and I gave her a lift in town once."

The sheriff turned to the rest of us.

"Any of you know her?"

"She called at Antigua this morning," Judge Drayton said, "to pay her respects to Mr. Cartwright. I talked to her a few minutes at the ball the other night."

"Today was the first I ever heard of her," Lawrence said.

Alec said, "I met her with my stepmother once, I think."

"I've seen her a few times at Pilgrimage houses, and to-day at the Draytons'," I said. "And once at the place where we got coffee after the ball. I've hardly more than said how do you do to her. Except at lunch yesterday—I forgot that."

I could see more men coming across the side garden to the bayou. One had a camera and flash equipment, and two of them were carrying a stretcher. Nobody said anything for a while, as they blundered down and up through the vines and came over to where we were standing.

The sheriff said, "What was she doing down here in the

first place?"

He looked around at us. "Does anybody know?"

Nobody did—or nobody said he did.

"Anybody any idea?"

Nobody had, apparently.

"Well, you can all go—except you, Heywood. I'll have to ask you to come along with me. I hate to do it, but you see what I'm up against."

"Yes, I see," Steve said quietly. "I'm ready."

"Just a minute, Jim," Judge Drayton said. He turned to me. I think I knew pretty well what was coming.

"Mrs. Gould," he said, very politely. "Where would you like us to send your bags? My niece will pack them for you, and we can have them to you in a very short time."

I had it coming to me, of course, and I wasn't really surprised at all.

"The hotel, I think, thank you, Judge Drayton," I said.

Steve interrupted. "You go to Tangiers, Louise."

I didn't like the tone of his voice. He'd had trouble enough with the Judge already without my adding to it.

"I'd better go to the hotel," I said.

"Send her things to Tangiers, please," he said.

"Very well, sir." Judge Drayton could not have been more urbane.

"I'll walk with you," Alec said. He took my arm with a "There, there," sort of squeeze, muttering something derogatory to his host's immediate ancestry under his breath.

"We'll go that way, if the sheriff doesn't mind," Steve said. "I'd like to pick up a toothbrush and introduce Mrs. Gould to Cousin Rose. We can take my car."

The sheriff nodded. "You hang around here, Joe," he said to one of his men. "The rest of you be careful, hear?"

Alec held out his hand to me. "I'll see you tomorrow," he said.

I could hear them crashing around in the bayou like an army on maneuvers. It occurred to me that maybe that was all right after all. Maybe the evidence they seemed bent on destroying ought to be destroyed—the way Anne and I had destroyed Miss Letty's footprint—if it was Miss Letty's. I'd never completely understood what Anne's apparent surprise had meant, or whether she was just pretending surprise.

I glanced back across the dark streak of the bayou at Antigua, wondering if she was watching us, and what Judge Drayton had said or done that had kept her from coming over with Miss Kate. Maybe she'd been packing my bag all this time. Whatever she was doing, wherever she was, I knew she must be sick with fear, hearing that cry, knowing—if she did know, and Miss Kate must have told her by this time—that Steve had been there.

Chapter Seventeen

DEATH AND TWO WILLS

THE SHERIFF WAS TALKING to Steve as we walked along.

"Which one of the Heywoods are you, by the way?" he was saying.

"My father is Elliot. He was Mr. Minot's first cousin."

"Did I hear you'd said something about a will?" Jim Bailey inquired. "You're not the one Mr. Minot left everything to if he married Miss Anne, are you?"

"I'm the one. And I want to marry her. Not on thát account."

"Well, I'll be damned. Excuse me, ma'am."

Bailey was silent for a few minutes.

"I sure wish I didn't have to do this," he said. I knew without seeing it that his good-natured, easy-going face was screwed up with perplexity.

"You don't think Lawrence would try to put anything over on you, do you? He's been courting Miss Ann all winter—in·between times. There's a lot of talk about old man Minot's plantations bein' right valuable some day."

Steve didn't say anything.

"You didn't hit that old lady on the head, did you, Heywood?"

Mr. Bailey sounded like a mother trying not to believe something about a wayward child that she knew was true.

"No, I didn't," Steve said.

"Well, what were you doin' down there?"

"I'd like to tell you, but I can't. I can tell you it didn't have anything to do with Mrs. Storm."

I saw Bailey glance at him. I guessed that—that being the case—he knew what Steve had been doing as well as I did. Anyway, he changed the subject immediately.

"What do you do for a living, Mr. Heywood?

"I am a captain in the air corps reserve. I've divided the last two years between advanced aeronautics at New Haven and a production job at the Hartford plant. I was a pilot with Pan-American a year before that. And right now I'm on my way to Kelly Field on a regular air corps assignment. Just stopped in Natchez to have a look at things. I'd better wire the Colonel I'm sticking around the jail a while so he won't wait breakfast for me."

I thought Jim Bailey had stopped to light a cigarette, but he hadn't. He'd just stopped.

"Good Lord, why didn't you say so in the first place?"

"Nobody asked me," Steve said. "I don't know what it's got to do with it, anyway."

"Good God, man! I can't put an officer in jail with a lot of trash."

"I don't see why not."

"Because I can't, that's all. I wasn't going to anyhow, as a matter of fact. None of the Heywoods ever been in jail that I know of. You'll be all right here at Tangiers to-night."

The sheriff mopped his forehead with his coat sleeve.

"You'll have to talk to the D.A. tomorrow, but we'll fix it up all right."

"I don't want anything fixed up for me," Steve said. His voice was quiet but dangerous. "The woman was murdered. If I didn't do it, somebody else did. The same thing's true of Mrs. Cartwright. Nobody's going to get away—"

"Shut up, Steve!" I said. "Mr. Bailey didn't mean that."

"That's right, ma'am." The sheriff spoke with dignity. "I was just tryin' to make it as easy for you as I can. I was right fond of old Mr. Minot. It was a big shock to me when we found him."

I suppose if I'd been a really bright person, or even had the intuitions that any woman's presumed to have, I'd have realized at this moment that the story of the Heywoods and the Draytons, which I'd fruitlessly puzzled my head so much about, was beginning to unravel. Steve's hand gripped my elbow so that I felt I ought to hear the bones crushing—and yet I doubt if he had any adequate idea of what was coming.

"What do you mean, found him?" he asked quietly.

Jim Bailey stopped again. "Haven't you heard?"

Steve shook his head. "I didn't know him. I saw him once when he came North years ago, I was in prep school then, and I was in college when he died. I didn't know there was anything unusual about it."

"I wouldn't say there was," Jim Bailey said deliberately. We started along again. "I guess it was shock. It was the night after they buried the old lady. She was a tartar. She had Mr. Minot and all the rest of 'em under her thumb from the day they were born."

"His mother?"

"No. His mother died when he was born. His grandmother. Eighty-nine and spry as a chicken, and tight— was she *tight!* She used to give Mr. Minot twenty-five cents on Saturday night—twenty-five cents. He worked like a dog running the plantations, and she'd hire a C.P.A. to go over the books to the last dime. They made good money, considering, but Mr. Minot never had a nickel, except that twenty-five cents."

"What happened?" I insisted.

"I guess it was the shock of being his own master. He came back from the funeral. Vidal Cutting—he's her lawyer—"

"I've seen him," Steve said.

"—he came out too. He read the will to Mr. Minot and Miss Rose and a couple of the others she'd kept with their nose to the grindstone. She left each of the rest five hundred dollars, and all the rest of it to Mr. Minot, saying what a fine boy he'd been and she hoped he'd get a good wife and raise a big family."

"How old was he then?"

"Fifty, I guess, and he looked sixty-five if he looked a day. Anyway, he just sat there stunned."

"He hadn't—I mean—" I didn't like to finish what I'd started.

"Killed her, you mean?"

"Something of the sort," I admitted.

"No, she died of lobar pneumonia. He was just stunned because he hadn't expected anything at all."

We'd reached the house and were sitting out on the back gallery steps. I could see the frost-white slates of Antigua's roof gleaming through the trees.

"Well, he got hold of himself, after a while, and the first thing he did, right away, was tell Vidal he wanted to make a will himself. And that's when *you* came in. Vidal told him he was crazy, and he said that was just the way he wanted it. They got a couple of people who'd come to clear up after the funeral to witness it."

Jim Bailey stopped and looked at us. "I don't know whether you're *interested* in this."

I swallowed, and Steve said, "Sure. Go on."

"Well, then he asked Vidal if he could lend him a couple of thousand dollars. Vidal still thought he was cracked, but he went out to get it. When he came back to tell him he could have it next morning, Mr. Minot was upstairs packing his bag. I guess the time you saw him was the only time he'd been out of Natchez since the war. He was excited, and he looked worn out. He was burning old papers and letters. The room was full of smoke—the old lady never let him have a fire in there. When I came—I was a deputy then—I remember there were three chimney swallows that got suffocated, I guess, and there they were lying in the burned papers right by his head. He'd got dizzy and fallen over on the hearth."

He pointed up behind us. "It was in that room right up

there."

We waited as he stopped for a moment.

"You could see where he'd caught hold of the mantel and knocked over a vase when he fell. There wasn't much blood. It was his heart, the doctor said. He'd just bled a little where his head hit the fire tongs. It was right pathetic, you know—his bag all packed, and the chimney swallows and him layin' there together, all of 'em dead. It was like the old lady had suffocated him the same as the swallows."

"There wasn't any doubt about it?" Steve asked after a while.

"No. We had to break in the door. The key was on the inside, lying on the floor. It dropped out when we broke it open. It was right sad. He'd been lookin' forward to gettin' away. He had a lot of road maps. The boys at the service station used to collect 'em for him from people. He had maps from tourist agencies and everywhere. Maybe they're still around."

We sat there silently. There wasn't a sound anywhere. The streamers of moss from the live oak moved softly back and forth, smoke-silvered in the moonlight.

"I guess he liked you being an aviator—maybe that's why he wanted you to marry Miss Anne. I remember there was a packet of circulars from all over tied with a piece of blue hair ribbon, and he'd written, 'Anne brought these,' on it. She used to sneak through the bayou and bring 'em to him. I guess she wrote every place for 'em, if she was only a kid."

"Why did she have to sneak through, Jim?" Steve asked.

"That's a long story, Steve."

I doubt if either of them was aware of the change in names, and of a new friendliness that seemed old and casual.

"That was before my time. As long as I can remember they've been at it like cats and dogs. Some say Mr. Minot wanted to marry Miss Kate and the old lady wouldn't let him. She was the one the murder in the bayou was about in sixty-four. She was eighteen then—she died in nineteen and thirty-five—but I guess she wasn't a good forgetter. Miss Kate's father was the one that killed her lover. Excuse me, ma'am. I forgot you were here."

"That's all right," I said.

"Yes, I guess that old bayou has seen a lot of things nobody knows much about," Jim Bailey said.

He got up abruptly, rather stiff all of a sudden, as if he regretted having let himself go the way he had. He looked at the gate. Anne's car was still nosed up against it. I realized with a start that the lights were turned off. I knew I hadn't done it.

"Isn't that Miss Anne's car?"

"Yes," I said. "I drove it over. I missed the turn at Antigua and got here instead. I'd just got here when I heard Mrs. Storm scream."

It didn't sound very plausible, but Jim Bailey didn't say anything. He was looking about with a puzzled look on his face. I suddenly thought of the dogs, and there must have been a kind of telepathy there, because Steve said, "I wonder where Cousin Rose's dogs are? They're usually raising hell."

"I was thinking about that," Jim said. "Oh, I know—somebody borrowed them for the fox hunt. They'll be back tomorrow."

He started off, and stopped. "Say, now—"

"Lucky coincidence," Steve observed.

"That's what I was just thinking myself. Darn lucky, the way they yap. Well, I'll get along."

"I'll take you," Steve said.

"No, thanks, I'd like the walk. Stick around till you hear from me, will you?"

They shook hands.

"Glad you came down, Steve. Wish you'd come back

and live here, when you're through the job we thought we finished last time."

"Thanks," Steve said. "I'll think about it."

"Good night, Mis' Gould."

He set off, and we stood watching him for a moment.

"Smarter than he looks," I said. "I hope."

"I hope, I hope," Steve added. "Nice guy, anyway. Do you want to go in, or do we wait for your bag?"

"We'd wait all night then, I'll bet," I said. "I'll borrow one of Millicent Storm's nightgowns. I don't suppose she'll mind."

"That," said Steve, "would not be decent. I'll lend you my extra pajamas."

We tiptoed, suddenly conscious of the hour, across the gallery to the old weatherbeaten door, and went inside. A single electric bulb hung from the cracked ceiling, glowing feebly out of a rose silk shade. In the gloom that was more dark than light I could make out a dingy loneliness that Antigua's grandeur couldn't possibly equal. As the front door closed behind us a gray-haired woman looked out of a room at the end of the hall. She started violently and stared at us, as well she might.

"This is Mrs. Gould, Cousin Rose," Steve said. He raised his voice, so I took it Miss Heywood was pretty deaf. "She's been at the Draytons, and Judge Drayton put her out—because of Anne."

Her face softened a little, I was relieved to see.

"I thought she could have the room that other woman was in."

Miss Rose wrapped her flannel bathrobe around her and came out into the hall.

"It's made up," she said. "I'm glad to have you come, but you'll have to be careful of the hot water. We don't have a great deal. I half expected somebody would come. A boy brought a bag over. I had him put it in the front room on the right."

"Thank you," I said. He must have brought it over before we came around to the front.

"They told me about that poor woman," Miss Rose said. "I've been afraid to go in her room. I wasn't here when it happened—I went to the movies with Cousin Elizabeth Hailey. Did they—"

Steve pulled at my sleeve, and we edged another step along.

"They don't know anything else, Cousin Rose. You go back to bed. We'll manage."

We hurried up the stairs. "This way," Steve said. He steered me to the door on the right near the small Palladian window.

"Isn't—this Mr. Minot's room?" I asked.

"He's been dead for years," Steve said. He nodded across the hall. "That was Mrs. Storm's room."

I think the same idea struck both of us at once.

"Maybe there's something—"

We both went across to it. Steve opened the door quietly.

"Wait a minute—the light's in the center."

He went across the room, stumbled against something and swore under his breath. I could hear him feeling his way. The room was black, the shutters all closed tightly.

"Here it is," he said. I heard a click as the light went on. For a moment we just stood there, both of us speechless, the droplight swinging in crazy, diminishing circles around his head.

Chapter Eighteen

TEAR-STAINED LETTER

THE ROOM WAS a shambles of disorder. Her clothes were scattered everywhere, her open suitcase trunk like Cornelia's was in the middle of the room where Steve had bumped against it, the drawers out and their contents strewed every which way. The pillows were on the floor, and a trail of pale-pink bath powder from a broken box had Steve's tracks in it as plain as a horsethief's trail in the snow. I'd never seen anything like it in all my life.

"You'd better go down and phone Jim Bailey right away," I said. "This will certainly hang you. Unless we can find a broom," I added. "Wait—there's her whisk broom. Give it to me, and take off your shoes—"

I stopped, a sick feeling hitting me a ghastly blow in the pit of the stomach. I looked up at him with a kind of growing horror I couldn't conceal.

"Steve!"

He looked back at me steadily.

"You mean, did I do it? The answer is no. The tracks just come this way, if you'll notice. I didn't do it. I thought you knew that."

"I'm sorry," I whispered. "I do, really. I don't know why —oh, well, let's skip it. You get out of that stuff and wash off the bottom of your shoes, and I'll brush it up."

"I'll phone Bailey," he said shortly. "If you thought that for a second, they'll all think it the rest of their lives. What do you suppose they were hunting for?"

I've never known why I did what I did just then. It was completely automatic. I didn't know I was doing it at all until it was too late. I put my hand in my pocket, pulled out my handkerchief, and held it out.

"For this," I said.

Miss Letty's locket lay in the center of the white linen square, the crumpled ribbon falling in a black festoon around it.

He looked at it, his face changing gradually from ordinary interest to bewilderment to astonished recognition, and back to bewilderment again.

"Well, where the *hell* did you get *that?*" he demanded.

"What is it?" I asked. "Do you—"

"Why, it's—"

He stopped and looked at me the way Anne had done that morning under the oak tree.

"Where did you get it?"

I looked at it myself, and back at him. "I don't know whether to tell you or not," I said dubiously. I was a little scared, as a matter of fact, at what I'd done.

"You might as well."

"It belongs to Miss Letty. Cornelia swiped it because she wanted to see what's in it. Millicent Storm thought it belonged to Cornelia, and she was over at Antigua this morning trying to buy it. It must have been what she was trying to find down in the bayou tonight."

I told him about what she'd said in her taxi, and what I'd said, and I told him about Miss Kate and the vase, too.

"What's in it?" he demanded.

I closed my hand over it and put it back in my pocket.

"That," I said, "is a secret."

He looked at my pocket a long time.

"It's no use," I said. "It's got blood on it—and if you're going to phone, you'd better go do it."

"I'm not going to," he said quietly then. "I'm going to clean this place up. You can help me if you want to."

It was some time later when I'd swept up the last of the powder on a newspaper. There was a long white-clouded feather where it had worked into the worn carpet, but I couldn't help that.

"They'll think she spilled it and tried to clean it up herself," I said. "I hope."

"Good thing the F.B.I. isn't in on it," Steve said coolly. He was in the doorway with his shoes under his arm, his coat streaked with powder, holding my shoes so they wouldn't get covered with the stuff. He tossed them to me. I put them on, turned out the light, and skirted around so I wouldn't pick up any of it. We looked back.

"I think it's a good job, on the whole," he said.

"It ought to be." It had taken us a full three-quarters of an hour. "I'm tired. I haven't done this much housework for years."

We started across the hall in front of the triple-arched window. It wasn't shuttered, because it was there for decoration chiefly, and the sashes were nailed down on the inside. The scene through it across the vine-shaded gallery was like something on an intimate Christmas card, with the late moon silvering everything with glistening frost. I'd started to say so when Steve halted abruptly and caught my arm. He bent forward, listening intently.

I stopped too, every nerve tense and sharpened, my heart chilling.

"What is it?" I whispered.

He straightened up. "I thought I heard something, outside. I'll have a look."

I don't know what had happened to me, but I was shaking, and my hands and feet were frozen. "No!" I said. "You're not either. If it is somebody, you'll get killed—and if it isn't it doesn't matter. Don't go—please don't!"

He gripped my shoulder. "Stop it, Louise! What's the matter with you? I won't go. Stop it, do you hear?"

He steadied me with a firm grip on my arm. "I'll just go down and lock the front door. All the windows are barricaded."

"Then let me come down with you," I said.

The idea of staying up there by myself was unbearable.

The whole place seemed alive with some dreadful static that set every nerve in my body taut with blind, unreasoning panic.

"Look," he said. "I'll turn on your light, and you go to bed. You're tired. That's all that's the matter with you. You've had a hell of a couple of days, and it's all backed up on you. Come along."

He led me across the hall and opened the door. Inside, leaning against the wall while he felt around for the light, I felt a little steadier. He turned it on, and I got across to the day bed at the foot of the great dismal four poster, and sat down, trying to pull myself together a little. *It must be something out in the hall,* I remembered thinking. I didn't seem to feel it so acutely in here.

He pulled the candlewick spread off the bed, pulled down the covers and put the pillows in place. Then he went over to the table, opened my small bag that Lusby had brought from Antigua, and put it on the day bed.

"Now you're all right. Lock your door if you want to. I'll stay downstairs—inside—until you get to sleep. If you wake up and get scared, just yell. I'll leave my door open."

"I'm all right," I said.

"I'll look under your bed, and in the wardrobe." He bent down. "Nothing here," he said. "And nothing here." He went over to the built-in cupboard, arched like the hall window, beside the fireplace. Both doors were locked.

"Good night, Louise," he said. "I'll leave the hall light on."

"Good night," I said. "Thanks—you're an angel."

"I'll tell you about Anne in the morning," he said. "You're going to be the only wedding guest."

"Oh, Steve, I'm delighted!" I said. "When?"

"Tomorrow night—if I'm not in jail. Good night."

And that, I thought, was why he'd whistled so happily folding up Millicent Storm's private garments and stowing them back in her suitcase. I took off my jacket and hung it in the wardrobe. And no wonder Judge Drayton had ordered me out of his house. Anne had probably been as transparent as Cinderella's slipper.

I began whistling a little, too. I'd forgotten all about my terror of a few minutes before. I went back to the day bed, sat down, took off my shoes, and felt around in my bag for my slippers. I fished them out, put one on, and had my toe in the other when I stopped short. There was something in it. I put my hand down and pulled out a crumpled envelope, sealed, with a faint flush of lipstick along the flap. I pulled out the letter inside it.

I read it through twice before I could really believe it. Maybe the blotched and blotted spots all over it were making me see it wrong.

Dearest Louise, it said. *I'm terribly sorry, but you'll know that without my telling you. Uncle Ed heard you talking to Steve on the telephone. He's never been so angry before. We didn't meet you because it was eleven o'clock before we even thought it was eight yet. We went to Tangiers and sat on the gallery because we didn't want to park out on the road. I thought it would be quicker to go back through the bayou. Steve came with me and Uncle Ed saw him. He was waiting just inside the door. He must have heard everything we said. Will you tell Steve it's all over? I can't marry him like I said I would. My uncle told me something I didn't know before. He's going to tell Steve, he said, but I don't want him to know, so tell him not to let my uncle tell him. He wouldn't like me any more. Please make him understand it's not my fault, it's just something nobody can help. Tell Steve I meant everything I said about loving him and feeling like I'd known him all my life, because I do. Please tell him for me, because I can't see him any more ever.*

She'd crossed out and blotted with her tears something there that I couldn't make out. The rest was a hurried scrawl.

They're coming back. Love, Anne.

Tell Steve I love him. I hope I've packed your things all right.

I read it through once more, a broken, vivid picture crying out through the tear-mottled blots of the childish purple ink. I got up and listened. I couldn't hear Steve downstairs, but I remembered he was in his stocking feet. And I had to show him that letter. I'd forgotten my fear of the hall out there—all I could think of was Anne.

I got up, ran to the door, and opened it.

I never even got his name out. There was a blinding flash of light, a shattering madhouse of crashing glass, a stinging, burning pain, a reeling and nauseating darkness with the floor flashing up to meet me—and nothing more.

Chapter Nineteen

SETUP FOR MURDER

I REMEMBER CRAWLING up slowly and horribly out of a sea-sick pit of oblivion, my head splitting, pain spraying through my whole left side, my arm aching and burning as if it were on fire. Through the waves of pain and nausea I became gradually aware of voices, one of them shouting, the other high-pitched and tremulous.

"I can't go myself—I don't dare leave her here alone! Put on your coat and run to the next house and phone for a doctor!"

It was Steve, and he was shouting to make Miss Rose understand. I struggled to make my rocking brain clear itself enough to work. *Why doesn't he just phone from here?* I remembered thinking, the back part of my mind appallingly clear all of a sudden. I moved my head a little. I was lying on the bed, my left arm stretched up high on a pile of pillows. I looked at it as if it were no longer a part of me, just something that I could feel shooting agony and staining everything red with blood. My hand was bluish-white and numb, and then I realized vaguely that part of the pain came from a tourniquet tied tightly around my arm.

I turned my head back, all of it horribly vivid again.

"It's perfectly safe for you!" Steve was shouting. "It's her they're after, not you! Go as fast as you can!"

I heard the door slam and her feet running frantically across the gallery and along the gravel. I closed my eyes, listening—listening as I'd never done before. The house was as still as death, and I was alone in it with Steve Heywood. As I heard him coming, my heart turned slowly to glacial rock. I could hear the stairs creak, and the dry wood of the old banisters creak. If he *had* killed Millicent Storm

—if it *was* he who'd shot at me— I closed my burning eyes and waited, measuring each step he had to take to bring him to my door, my body rigid and paralyzed, my burning arm no longer a part of me but something remote and impersonal.

I suppose I was a little delirious too, because through another door in the room—and then it wasn't this room at all but my own living-room at home—I saw Tom come in with his bag in his hand, completely fagged. He shook his head and said, "The rest of it's up to God—I've done all I can." I opened my eyes and started to speak to him, but he was gone, and the other door—the door of the room I was really in—was opening softly, and Steve was coming in.

I closed my eyes then, so that I could just see him through the blur of my lashes, thankful for the dingy bed curtains that shielded me from the light. His face was a white blob, grim as iron, and his eyes were bright—too bright—and haggard. He came slowly to the foot of the bed. I could hear the boards crack under the carpet. He stopped a moment, and came along to the side of the bed. It was exactly as if I'd left my body, somehow, and was sitting cross-legged on the floor, watching him. He stopped, and stood looking down at me.

"Louise?" he whispered.

I didn't move. I just waited.

He put his hand slowly in his pocket. And somehow I wasn't afraid any longer. *Maybe this is what death is like,* I thought, *—young and strong and hard as steel, and unhappy too.* Because his face was so bitterly unhappy then that I knew if he was going to kill me it wasn't because he wanted to. There was something so impersonal about it that it didn't seem to be me, or him—it was just two circumstances that had got in each other's way. It wouldn't make any more sense than Cornelia's murder had made, or Millicent Storm's.

I could see his hand moving out of his coat pocket—and

then I saw Anne's letter in it. He was just looking at it, so that I knew he'd already read it; and then he turned away as slowly as he'd come, putting it back in his pocket again. I still didn't move. I had no emotion really, but just the same kind of detached feeling, waiting to see what would happen—like a spectator on the roadside, and a fox in the bayou at the same time, I suppose.

I saw him straighten up suddenly and look across the room at the fireplace. Then he went across to the locked cupboard at the side of it. He put his hand into his pocket and brought it out, and I saw a key in it and turned my head so I could watch him more easily and saw one cupboard door swing open, and then the other. The shelves were piled with bundles of papers three or four inches wide.

Mr. Minot's road maps and travel folders, I thought calmly.

The cupboards evolved some way in my mind into long stretches of sky and sea and lands thousands of distant miles that he'd never seen but had traversed in his dreams. The spaces between the shelves were stacked full of them, except on the middle shelf in the center where two small bundles lay side by side.

I saw Steve reach in and take one of them and look at it, holding it up to read something written on the paper he pulled out from under the ribbon that tied it. After a minute he put that one back and took out the one beside it. He looked at it for an instant as if it didn't make the same obvious sense as the other, and then went on through the cupboard, looking at the cover of each bundle. Among them I recognized the color and format of a well-known oil company's road map. At the last one he stopped, looked around, drew it out and opened it up. He looked at it for a long time, folded it again and put it back in place with the others, and then put the whole bundle in his inside pocket, and stood there looking abstractedly down at the hearth.

After a moment he turned and looked at the door. It was a curious pantomime that I was watching, lying there in the shadow of the bed curtains. It was like a grotesque game of parlor charades with the actor unconscious of his audience. He turned back, put his hand on the mantel and stood there for a moment, looking down at the hearth. Then he reached down and picked up the wrought-iron fire tongs, and held them for a moment. They clattered a little as he put them into place. A moment later he was looking at the door again.

If it had been a game, I would have said—I could feel myself vaguely thinking—*Oh, I know—it's Mr. Minot you're thinking about, and you're thinking some one killed him with the fire tongs—but you've forgotten the door was locked, and the key was lying on the floor inside.* But, of course, it wasn't a game; it had a ghostly kind of reality that had no relation to a game of any sort. And then I saw he was thinking the same thing. If some one had killed Mr. Minot, there was still the fact of the key on the inside of the door. I could see him thinking that, in the puzzled frown that appeared on his face. He stood there a moment longer, then went across to the door and took the old iron key out of the lock. He went outside and pulled the door shut behind him.

I watched, with a kind of horror growing over me. *What is he doing?* I thought. I heard the scraping sound of iron on wood, and sat up, my head swimming dizzily. I stared over the foot of the bed. Then I heard the sound again, and stared down at the crack under the bottom of the old door. Slowly, and really terribly, the head and then the shank of the key appeared, moving under the door—and then with a sudden movement it shot out onto the carpet.

Steve opened the door. The key was lying there just as if it had dropped from the lock. He stood looking down at it.

"Steve!" I gasped.

He whirled around, and stared at me as if I were Mr. Minot come back from the grave.

"Do you mean somebody—killed him, too?" I whispered.

I sank back on the pillows as he wavered before me in a foggy darkness, my head swimming with nausea. He came across the room quickly, took my hand and held it tight. I was conscious of the burning pain in my arm, and then something slipped down my face and was salty when my tongue touched my lips, and I knew I was crying. And I knew it was because now I knew it wasn't Steve who'd shot at me in the dingy shadowy hall of Tangiers.

I heard myself whispering again, "Was he *killed,* Steve?"

He looked down at me for a moment. "I think so," he said. "Nobody could prove it, now. Lie still. I hear them coming. We'll talk about it later. And listen—don't say a thing about that room over there. Under any circumstances. Do you hear?"

He went out to meet them. I lay there trying to figure out what he meant. I couldn't understand it. Did he still believe, as I believed, that it had been Miss Letty hunting for her locket? Or did he know something I didn't know? Or could he possibly have no thought of connecting that mess we'd cleaned up with Millicent Storm's murder and the attempt to kill me? Much as I didn't like to think that Miss Letty was trying to murder me, there was certainly an extraordinary combination of circumstances. Cornelia swiped the locket and was killed. Miss Letty went through her belongings with careful and painstaking thoroughness. Her footprint—I still believed it was hers—was on the bank above Cornelia's body. Millicent Storm had seen the locket and had wanted it, and she was dead—and her things had been as thoroughly if not as painstakingly gone through.

And then I'd showed Steve the locket, and he'd said he

heard the sound on the gallery, and I'd been shot, from outside the gallery window—and there was no doubt of any sort in my mind that it was me that was being shot at, because earlier we'd both stood there by the window, perfect targets. It all seemed to follow the locket, in some way. Both Steve and Anne had acted so oddly when they saw it, and so had Miss Kate Drayton when she heard about it.

I was thinking all that, vaguely and painfully, when I heard the voices in the hall, and then in a minute they were in the room—Steve and Jim Bailey and another man I didn't know.

"This is Doctor Richards, Louise," Steve said.

The doctor was brisk and businesslike and quite nice about being routed out of bed.

"Hold the light, Bailey," he said. "Did you apply this tourniquet, Heywood? Good job—you saved her life. I'll keep it on a while. I want some water boiled."

Then it seemed to me that hours passed, hours punctuated by Jim Bailey's going out into the hall and standing there looking at the window through which I'd been shot, and coming back and looking at me, with heavy troubled lines in his face, and going out again, and coming back, until I thought I'd go mad. Then there were hours, it seemed to me, of prodding and poking and cutting, mixed with vaguely familiar words bringing my husband back again, about "grazed radial artery—easily ligated—artery clamps—tie off the vessel." And at last there was the relief as he took off the tourniquet, and then my arm was clean and white and bandaged and very comfortable, and the doctor smoothed my hair back gently from my forehead and said, smiling, "You're more scared than hurt. All blood and no bones. I'll be around in the morning. Take it easy for a week or two with that arm. I'll call your husband and tell him about it. Mr. Heywood tells me he's a doctor."

I don't know whether all three of them stayed there the

rest of the night or not. I could hear them out in the hall until everything became blurred, and when I woke up in the morning they were all there.

Doctor Richards looked at his thermometer. "That's a girl," he said. "Your husband's taking a plane down tomorrow. He'd have come today but he had a case, and I told him you were all right."

He turned to the sheriff, standing awkwardly in the doorway. "You can talk to her, but don't wear her out."

Jim Bailey scratched his head. Then he came over and put the morning paper on my lap.

Second Club Woman Murdered. Third Wounded. Sheriff Baffled!

The huge headlines screamed across the whole top third of the page.

Doctor Richards looked at it with a gleam in his eye. "It looks like they've got something there, Jim," he said.

"I'm not baffled, I'm stumped," Jim Bailey said gloomily. "I figured you could give us some kind of a steer, maybe, Mis' Gould. Do you know any reason anybody'd have for murderin' a lot of club women?"

Only Miss Letty's locket, I thought—but I shook my head. Then I looked up at Steve. He was grinning like the village idiot, and Doctor Richards was smiling ironically.

"I know what you fellows are thinkin'," Jim Bailey said. "But that's not what I mean. This is serious. Good God, if some maniac's loose murderin' club women, it'll ruin Natchez. It's club women that put us on the map again. My wife's one."

"But it's only *visiting* club women, Jim," Doctor Richards said.

"That's the idea," the sheriff said doggedly. "It's the visitors that make the Pilgrimage. We've got to get to the bottom of this."

It was a little reassuring that we were a civic problem, Cornelia and Millicent and I, not merely a criminal or legal one. We had to be solved, so as not to frighten tourists away and ruin business. I wondered vaguely if they could sue us for damages if receipts fell off.

"Of course we've got to find out who did it anyway," Jim said. He looked at me. "There's one thing I'd like to ask you, Mis' Gould," he said reluctantly. "I gathered last night you were having some sort of trouble with the Judge?"

I nodded.

"What was it about?"

I looked at Steve.

"Go ahead, tell him," he said.

I don't know why I hadn't realized before the effect that Anne's letter had had on him. Perhaps because he'd concealed it so well up to then. It was there now, in the lines of his jaw and eyes.

"Judge Drayton thought I'd been helping Steve and Anne see each other," I said. "And correctly, I'm afraid. He didn't like it."

Jim nodded.

"That doesn't help us much. The other ladies didn't have anything to do with it, did they?"

"No," I said.

He shifted about uneasily, and finally got up to go. "Well, don't you worry, Mis' Gould," he said, with what seemed to me a remarkable lack of any real confidence. "We'll see you're taken care of all right."

When he'd gone Steve came over and sat on the foot of the bed.

"Now we can get down to business," he said. "How do you feel?"

"Rotten, thanks."

"Good. Now you see this whole business has become as simple as pie?"

"No," I said. "I don't."

He nodded seriously. "It's perfectly obvious. All you

have to do is use your head. You know something that's
so damned dangerous to somebody that he's willing to risk
a second murder in one night to keep it from getting out.
Now what is it?"

"You tell me," I said. "I'd like to know."

He shook his head.

"That shot wasn't aimed at me. If I'd known anything,
he could have got me when we were standing there. He
was just outside on the gallery—cut the telephone wires
first. Must have climbed up."

"Unless, of course," I said, "he—or she—was in the
house already, and went out by one of the windows—in
Mrs. Storm's room, say."

He looked at me through the haze of smoke from his
cigarette. "What do you mean by that?" he asked quietly.

"Look, Steve," I said. "Wouldn't it be simpler if I just
told you everything, from the beginning?"

"All right. Shoot."

"Don't say that," I said.

"All right—tell me all, Mrs. Gould, if you please."

Chapter Twenty

SUMMONS FROM THE PAST

I DID. I BEGAN at the beginning with Miss Letty's not want-ing to come down, and I went all the way through the busi-ness of Miss Kate and the locket and Mrs. Storm's saying, "Do you think she could have lost it in that ditch?" and my saying, "Probably."

"And what I'd like to know now, if you don't mind, is *what* you were doing out under the magnolia tree. Because it *was* you, wasn't it?"

He looked at me blankly. *"Me?* What would I be doing under a magnolia tree in the moonlight all by myself? It wasn't me."

"But after you ran, I saw your car come in the drive over here!"

"Not after *I* ran, because I didn't run, Mrs. Gould. When I left you and Anne I drove around I don't know how long."

He tossed his cigarette across the room into the fireplace, missed it, got up and kicked it in.

"She was something I guessed I must have dreamed about," he said slowly. "I felt like a dirty, lowdown bum, talking the way I had at the ball."

For a moment we both forgot the man under the mag-nolia tree.

"What are you going to do, Steve? You got her letter, didn't you?"

He nodded. "Poor little devil," he said. "I'd like to—oh, well."

"You mean you're just going to take it?" I demanded hotly.

"You keep your shirt on, sister. I'm not going to make it

any worse hell for her than it is now, until I can get her away. You leave that to me. I said I was going to marry her and that's that. None of those so-and-so's are going to stop me."

"But if she goes out and marries Alec just to get away—"

"I'll—"

He stopped abruptly. Before I knew what had happened, really, he was across the room and out the door, and then I heard the swift click of heels coming up the hanging staircase.

"Anne!"

"Steve!"

I knew they were in each other's arms, clinging together. The almost desperate yearning in their voices as they'd met, crying each other's name, made me catch my breath. I hadn't realized that they'd gone quite so far in being in love.

"Where is she, Steve—is she very bad?"

For a moment he didn't answer. I could see that my health wasn't of much importance just then.

"She's fine," he said. "Listen—I love you, Anne. I'm figuring some way—"

"Oh, don't!" she said. "Please—you mustn't! I can't, Steve, I can't! Where is she! I've got to see her. I can't stay but a minute—they'll find out I've gone."

"You're not going back at all," Steve said. "They can send your things, too. You're going to stay with me."

"Oh, I can't, Steve! You don't *understand!*"

"I understand I'm in love with you, and you're going to marry me, and the hell with everything else," he said calmly. "Now come on and see Louise, and shut up. You said you'd let me have this house, and you'll do as I say in it—"

"Oh, don't make me feel any more unhappy than I am already!"

"I'm sorry," he said. "She's in here."

They came in my room.

"Louise!"

"It's practically nothing at all," I said.

"I was so scared," she said softly. "Whoever could have—"

"That's what we're trying to find out," Steve remarked. "And we're not getting along very well."

I saw a shadow come over his face. He could very well have added, "But your Aunt Letty's the best bet so far."

"I can't understand it," Anne said. "If there was anybody in town who'd known any of you before you came— But there wasn't."

We didn't say anything to that.

"The only people who knew Mrs. Cartwright were Mrs. Storm and you—and Aunt Letty, of course, and Steve, in a way. And Lusby."

Steve and I glanced at each other. She was saying·it the way a child does who's repeating something heard at the family dinner table.

"But now that you and Mrs. Storm are out of it, and Lusby's out, because he was at Mamie's with Isaac last night after he brought Alec's things out to the house—"

"It leaves your Aunt Letty and Mr. Steven Heywood," Steve said.

"But that's ridiculous."

Two bright spots deepened under her long sweeping lashes.

"Where was your aunt last night, by the way, Anne?" Steve asked gently.

"At home."

She wasn't telling the truth, and she didn't lie very well, I thought. And I knew then that it was Miss Letty who'd rifled Millicent's room. She moved back a step.

"I've got to go. I just came to see how you were, Louise. If there's anything I can do—"

She stopped abruptly. A car was coming in the driveway. She ran to the window and looked out, her face turning as white as the counterpane on my bed. Then she looked around in sudden panic.

"It's my uncle!" she whispered. "What *can* I do?"

Steve got up. I didn't much like the way he looked. "Sit down," he said. "I'll talk to him."

"No, Steve—please!"

She flashed around at him. "Please don't! Don't you care anything about me at all? *Please!*"

He went over to her, took her shoulders in his hands and looked down at her steadily. Her eyes were wide and pleading.

"Look, Anne," he said quietly. "He can't tell me anything that will make any difference in the way I feel about you. Don't you know that?"

There was a sharp imperative rap on the front door.

"I'm going down there. Just be quiet. I love you very much, little girl. And you love me too, don't you?"

The door downstairs opened. I could hear Judge Drayton's cold voice. "Anne? Anne?" I saw it send a terrified shiver through the girl's body.

"Oh, yes!" she whispered.

He bent down and kissed her on the forehead.

"Don't forget it, will you?"

She stood there, white and shaken, her hands dropped woodenly to her side. Then she turned and came unsteadily over to the bed, her face haggard and her eyes listless, all the life and brilliance drained out of them.

"It's no use. He'll tell him anyway. He said he was going to."

"Look, Anne," I said gently. "You're being ridiculous—aren't you? Don't you know that nothing is ever as awful to anyone else as it seems to you?"

"This isn't only me," she said.

She was staring abstractedly in front of her, not seeing anything, like a mask of tragedy.

"You don't know my uncle. He doesn't care who he

hurts. If it were just me I wouldn't care—not so much."

I didn't say anything, because it was hard to know what to say. Unless she wanted to tell me, I didn't want to know —though I had an idea that if she could tell someone it might get that glazed look of despair out of her eyes. She didn't seem aware of me any more. She didn't even look up when some one tapped on the door.

I said, "Come in." It was the incredibly old and decrepit colored woman who'd brought my breakfast.

"Miss Anne?"

Anne looked up. "Good morning, Martha."

"Th' Judge say he'd like you to come down in th' parlor. He say he'd like th' other lady, too, if she is able."

She closed the door. Anne sat there with her hands folded tightly together, steadying herself. Then she got up.

"You don't feel like coming, do you?"

I didn't, but there was something so poignant in the way she said it that I hesitated.

"It would be easier," she said. "He doesn't like you, but you're a stranger. It might—"

"Give me that skirt, and the stockings," I said. "And that sweater. Cut the sleeve. There are some nail scissors. I can make it all right. And my lipstick. And that scarf for a sling."

She got my things and took down my jacket from the wardrobe. "You'd better put this around you. You don't want to catch cold."

"There's not much danger of that," I said. I'd developed a slow-burning resentment against the arrogant imperiousness of that old man downstairs that would have kept me warm in a bathing-suit in Labrador. It certainly got me downstairs and into the parlor. Whether it was going to keep me from slipping off the brown horsehair Victorian sofa with the springs sticking into me at various extraordinary angles, I wasn't quite so sure.

"Sit down, Anne," Judge Drayton said coolly. He'd

given me a very formal bow, as I came in.

I've often wondered if all this could have happened in any other surroundings—if the parlor hadn't been so completely Victorian, from the carved rosewood Belton set of brown horsehair to the spicy smell of pot pourri mixed with mold and sickening sweetness. I had a vague impression of marble-topped tables and wax flowers and fruit under glass, faded carpets, and long-dead Heywoods hanging dingily on the walls. If the room had been light and full of glass and air and color, Judge Drayton wouldn't have had the power he had. It was a dead room. The dead past was there, returned to life, withering youth and love with its fleshless iron hand.

"Sit down, Heywood," Judge Drayton said.

"I'll stand, if you don't mind."

At any other time, I think, seeing him leaning against the corner of the mantel, with the pair of stuffed bluejays and a branch of wrought-iron leaves just over his head, would have seemed rather funny. It didn't now. Nothing seemed funny—not even the grotesque shell-and-wax funeral wreath framed over the piano, with the center angel unglued and standing on his head in a pile of sea shells and grapes at the bottom of the box frame. It was all too real. Anne sat with her head up, her eyes straight ahead, her scarlet lips incongruously cut across her dead-white face.

Chapter Twenty-One

Power of a Secret

"I AM ASSUMING that in your different ways," Judge Drayton said coldly, "you are both fond of my niece, and that neither of you would willfully injure her. That is why I have decided to tell you this."

He looked at Steve, and at me.

"Only five people now alive have known it. Anne herself did not know until last night."

His eyes rested on mine again. If you have ever looked into a deep pond with a thin coat of ice over it, and the ground around it barren and hard with frost, you'll know how he looked just then. Anne's hands tightened in her lap. As she looked at him I had a sudden desire to cry out to him, and tell him to stop—he didn't know what he was losing, what was dying in her face. It seemed to me he couldn't be realizing that she was seeing him suddenly with adult eyes, just as he was, not with a child's eyes any longer. The illusion was breaking down, and I could see it breaking, and nothing could ever build it up again. She was perfectly calm now; all the panic and the distress were gone. He couldn't hurt her now, I thought. It was just himself he was hurting.

"Anne's name is not Drayton," he said evenly, to Steve. "My brother died childless. Anne has no name. Your father's cousin, Minot Heywood, was her father. He was betrothed to my sister Kate. He deserted her and ran off like a thief in the night—lower than a thief—with my sister Laetitia. We brought Anne back to Antigua, a nameless—"

Steve cut him short with a swift move forward, his eyes hard and dangerous and burning.

"That's enough," he said quietly. "You brought her back, and you gave her her mother's name. She had a right to it. But if she had to make up a name, what of it? What's that got to do with her? She's going to take her father's name now, because it's my name too—and I'm proud to give it to her."

He came across the room and took Anne by the hand, and stood with his arm around her, holding her close to his side.

"Why do you tell her now? If nobody knew—"

Judge Drayton had risen, his face gray as death. "Because you are a Heywood!"

His cold voice cut across Steve's protest like a whip lashing through the air.

"She'll never have the name Heywood. Never—do you hear?"

Anne's body quivered, Steve's arm tightened around her. I watched him draw his breath slowly in and let it out slowly, controlling his desire to go across the room and do God knows what to the bitter, terrible old man standing there, erect and merciless. Both of them were silent, and there was no other sound in the room.

Judge Drayton sat down.

"You came here to get the Heywood plantations," he said quietly. "You may have them, if you have the effrontery to take them. They belong to Anne. The great wrong that Minot Heywood had to redress, for his soul, was the wrong he'd done to her and her mother. The wrong he did my sister Kate he could never redress. In a court of law in Mississippi, Anne's claim would hold before yours. But we have no desire to publish her mother's shame to the whole world."

It is only in this room that that would have validity, I thought desperately.

"I asked you never to say that again," Anne said quietly. "She must have loved him very much. I loved him too, and he loved me. It wasn't his fault. I'm glad he was my father —glad, do you hear?"

"I think the less melodrama the better," Judge Drayton said coldly. "It has nothing to do with it."

"Nor have the plantations," Steve said. "Anne is going to marry me, Judge Drayton. She will have them without any discussion of any kind."

"I have told you Anne is not going to marry you."

"I don't know just how you're going to stop her," Steve said coolly.

Judge Drayton's eyes were like Miss Letty's the night she flew at Cornelia.

"I will tell you, Mr. Heywood. I realize that standards in your part of the country are different from what they are in the South. But I don't believe they are lax enough to overlook an irregularity of this importance."

Anne closed her eyes again, and straightened her body, erect as a young pine tree. She opened them, and looked at him, waiting, her hand clasped in his, his arm still around her, holding her tightly.

"It's a chance we're willing to take, Judge Drayton," he said evenly.

"But I doubt if it is a certainty that you'd be willing for your children to take—or that my sister Laetitia's friends would even consider taking."

"You mean you would publish it to the world, I take it?"

"I do, indeed."

"In that case, there's nothing we can do about it," Steve said.

"Nothing," said Judge Drayton. "I'm glad you have sense enough to see it, sir."

"Thank you. The telephone line is fixed now. Would you like me to call a reporter from the evening paper? He can announce our engagement at the bottom of the column."

Judge Drayton looked at him calmly. "If you wish, Mr. Heywood."

Anne unloosed her fingers from Steve's and moved out of the protecting circle of his arm.

"No," she said quietly. "I won't let you hurt my— mother. You haven't told her—have you?"

"I told you last night I would never tell her that any one knew—as long as you act in accordance with my wishes."

"You mean as long as I don't marry Steve."

"Or have anything to do with him."

"Then if you don't tell her, I won't marry him," Anne said. "I'll promise that. I've never made you a promise I haven't kept. But I won't marry Lawrence. And I won't marry Alec. I take it the reason my mother is so shabby and so poor is that she's always paid for me at Antigua, and that what I thought was my father's share of the place was hers. I should be grateful to you, but I'm not. I see what she meant the other night. She was right. Mr. Minot is dead, and you can't hurt him. It's only the living you can hurt. I'd like you to go now."

He looked at her silently, with a slow dawning incredulousness. Then his whole face closed like a trap, absolutely expressionless.

"You're coming with me," he said.

"I'll come when I'm ready," she replied calmly. "I've given you my promise."

He looked at her for a moment. Then he said, "Very well, Anne. I've also given you mine. Let us hope neither of your friends will be misguided enough to take matters in their own hands."

He bowed to me. "Good-by, Mrs. Gould."

"Good-by, Judge Drayton," I said.

He walked past Steve to the door and out, closing it firmly behind him.

"Anne!"

"No, Steve!"

She moved quickly so that he couldn't take her in his arms again.

"It wouldn't be right. I've promised. Oh, don't you see, Steve? She's suffered so much because of me—I couldn't let her be hurt again. Oh, you *do* see, don't you?"

He went back to the fireplace and stood there looking down into it. Then he turned around.

"I see," he said. "For the present anyway."

He hesitated an instant.

"There's one thing you'd like to know. It might make it a little easier."

"I don't feel—branded, or ashamed, Steve," she said gently. "It's just that I don't want her to—again."

"That's what I mean," he said. "You remember all the road maps and travel folders he used to collect?"

She nodded. "I used to spend most of my allowance on stamps to get them for him."

"Well, it wasn't because he wanted to take a lot of trips. There was only one trip he was going to take."

"What do you mean?"

He put his hand in his pocket, took out the bundle he'd taken from Mr. Minot's cupboard the night before, and slipped the rubber band off it.

"I think he took all the maps people brought him just so he could pick out the ones he wanted," he said. "And they've all got one route marked—or alternate routes all going to the same place."

He unfolded the Mississippi map that was on top and laid it on the table. "The mileage is marked. It goes up to Nashville, see? Then it goes on in Tennessee."

He opened the next one. "This goes up through Ohio."

Then he laid one open on top of the others and ran his finger along the red crayon that Mr. Minot Heywood had used to mark his route. "They all stop here."

Anne and I leaned over and looked at the tiny dot encircled with a broad red line.

"Brentwood!" Anne exclaimed. "Why, that's—that's where Aunt Letty—that's where she lives!"

Steve nodded.

"It was where he was packing his bags to go the night—"

The night he was murdered, I thought.

"—he was taken ill and died."

Anne stood looking down at it a long time. When she raised her face to Steve her eyes were shining with tears.

"The first minute he was free," she whispered. "The first minute he could call his soul his own. Oh, Steve, I'm so glad! I'm so very, very glad!"

"I'm glad, too," he said gently. But there was a twinge of bitterness in his voice, too, and I knew it meant that while he was glad, he wanted there to be some way to punish the person, whoever it was, who had kept Minot Heywood from making that trip he'd planned for so long. He folded the maps one by one and put them back in his pocket.

"Do you think I might show them to—to her, so she'd know too?" Anne asked softly.

Steve shook his head. "I wouldn't—not now. She might guess. Well, come along—I'm going to take you home."

He took her hand.

"There are a lot of things I want to say—so you'll remember this isn't the end—it's just the beginning, for you and me."

He looked at me then, and remembered, I suppose. "No, I guess I'd better stay here."

"No. Don't be silly," I said. "Go on. I'll be all right."

Anne looked at me with a kind of dawning horror in her eyes.

"You mean—you think they'll try— Oh, Louise, how awful. Oh, no, Steve—you mustn't leave her! Oh, how horrible!"

I glanced past them through the window. "There's someone coming now," I said. "Maybe it's Jim. He can stand guard a while. After all, I'm his problem."

"You're ours, too," Steve said. He went over to the window and looked out. A car had stopped at the gate.

"It's not Jim," he said.

Anne looked out. She put her hand on Steve's arm quickly.

"It's Alec," she said. "He's got a different car. They've sent him over after me! Louise—you've got to tell him I've gone! Aunt Letty said he was going to ask me something today, and I don't—I can't listen, not now."

"All right," I said. "Quick, both of you. Go out that way through the garden. He can stay with me till you get back, Steve. I haven't had a chance to talk to him, anyway."

As they went out I managed to get to the window. Alec had left his car in the road and was coming through the gate. It was too bad, really, I thought. If it hadn't been for Steve, it would have been his suit I was backing. With Cornelia out of the way he'd have made a grand husband for any girl, and Anne would have come to Brentwood to live.

I listened for the back door to close on her and Steve, and heard it just as Alec knocked. I waited for the old colored woman to answer, knowing that Miss Rose, if she was anywhere about, would never hear it, and when she didn't, I raised my voice. "Come in, Alec—I'm in here."

Chapter Twenty-Two

DIRECTIONS FOR MURDER

HE CAME. "Hello, what's this I hear, and how are you?" Good Lord. Have you talked to Tom?"

He looked at me curiously.

"Doctor Richards did," I said. "He's flying down tomorrow. Sit down and talk to me a while. Is there any news?"

He sat down across from where Judge Drayton had sat, and looked around. He seemed a little nervous.

"Dismal hole, isn't it?"

I nodded.

"The Judge said Anne was over here," he said.

"She's been gone quite a while. But don't go. I haven't had a chance to talk to you since you've come."

"Steve here?"

I started to say where Steve was, and then I thought maybe I'd better not. The Judge might have sent him over for exactly that purpose.

"He's around somewhere," I said. "Have you found out anything new?"

"I've been talking to Bailey and the doctor," he said. "The doctor said the bullet grazed the artery in your arm."

I nodded and held it out in the sling.

"I'm all right—I just have to be careful with it. I don't want the artery to come untied," I said.

I had to think of something to talk to him about, until Steve got back. A kind of odd panic at being left alone began to seep through my insides. I could feel my hands, or maybe just my feet, getting colder by the moment.

"I wonder which one of the Heywoods that is," I said, nodding up at the dingy portrait over the mantel.

Alec got up to look at it, and turned around and looked

at me sharply.

"What's the matter?" I asked.

"Is this—that locket?" he said queerly.

I felt something inside me turning slowly into a cold gray jelly. I got up. Or at least I started to get up, and there seemed to be something holding me there in my chair. I looked up at the portrait. In the blackened canvas I could see a woman's head and bare shoulders. On her full bosom, cracked and dulled with time, I could see that golden egg-shaped ornament, hanging on a black ribbon around her throat. I couldn't see the spray of jeweled lilies of the valley, but I knew they were there just as surely as I knew the locket itself was tucked away in the pocket of my coat lying around my shoulders.

I leaned back in the chair, the carved flowers in its rosewood frame hard against my hand. I was sick and dizzy. And then, as I sat there, looking from the old portrait to Alec Cartwright standing in front of it, still looking queerly at me, it was all there—the whole picture whirled and settled into shape, blinding and nauseating and with a kind of terrible clarity. And I prayed, *Oh, God, what shall I do?*

It hadn't come in a flash, the way some things come—for I'd really known it all the time, just as Steve said I'd known it. Now it was there in my mind, clear as the table in front of me, clear and certain as death. For death was there in the room with me, too, his icy fingers closing around my heart. I knew perfectly well—I'd known it from the beginning—that Alec Cartwright had killed Cornelia. He had killed Millicent Storm. He had tried to kill me—and now he had come back to do it properly.

I kept my eyes fixed on the gold locket in the portrait. It was like a beacon in the seething blackness of some raging storm-tossed night. I had to keep my eyes on it to keep my sanity.

Steve, Steve! Come back now!

It was a silent cry, desperate beyond belief. Alec Cartwright was saying something. I didn't hear it, but I could hear myself answering him, my voice natural and detached as if the body it was in wasn't my body but someone else's, some third person in the room who had no knowledge of Alec, who felt none of the cold breath and closing fingers of death. And I mustn't let that voice become confused with me, I thought. I must go on talking, not letting him be sure, letting him waver between doubt that I really knew whatever it was I knew, and the certainty and fear he had that I did know. *He won't kill me while I'm talking to him,* I thought. *He really likes me—he doesn't in his heart want to kill me. He wants to be sure Steve isn't upstairs, won't come barging in if I should have time to scream.*

He spoke again, and again my voice answered him.

It takes so long to say it all in words, but in my mind— the mind apart from the casually-speaking tongue—it was spread out like a block of print that my eyes could take in all in one quiet glance. Alec Cartwright had the only motive for killing Cornelia—her penury, her miserliness, where he was concerned as well as with everybody else, with only her death standing between him and his father's estate. But that wasn't how I'd known; it wasn't what had broken down the threshold so that memory functioned at just that moment. It was the locket. He must have seen it that night—threw it down, probably, into the bayou after her. And probably he'd just asked that to see if I knew.

Then I thought of his phone call to Cornelia, and her surprise and annoyance, and his saying to me when he came that night, "I thought you'd gone home. I thought the Pilgrimage was over"—and then last night, as we'd stood by Millicent Storm's body, with Judge Drayton and Steve quarreling about the oil on Mr. Minot's plantations, and he'd said, "That must be what she meant," and then the silence before he said, "She telegraphed me." But she'd only known it the night before her death—after the candlelight ball, when she'd overheard Lawrence and Judge Drayton talking in the dining-room. She hadn't telegraphed him. She'd told him, just before he murdered her —she'd told him that if he wanted money, that was the way to get it. "That's the kind of girl I'd like my stepson to marry," she'd said, that morning.

And Alec would know about the revolver—she'd always had one in the car—and he was the only person who would know it. The car had stood out in front of Antigua all the night before. And he'd been there, under the magnolia tree. I'd thought it was Steve when I saw him running, because there was something vaguely familiar and recognizable about him, and I'd thought Steve was the only young man I knew in town, and his car coming in had seemed to prove it.

And then I knew I'd already seen Alec Cartwright that night. So had Millicent Storm. She'd sealed her death warrant when she said, "I never forget a face. I recognized you the first time I saw you." And I'd sealed mine afresh—almost—when I said, "I saw her at the service station where you get the sandwiches after the ball." It was Alec who'd driven up behind me and Steve, by the oil truck, and sat with his car parked next to Millicent's. It had been enough, probably, when he'd told me Cornelia had telegraphed him, because he'd made a mistake then that he knew I'd think about sometime—but if I'd been at the service station too it was just a double danger.

He'd come up out of the bayou with Lawrence, and he hadn't been in the house at all. He'd not had time; he'd just fallen in with Lawrence and come back. And then, knowing that sooner or later I must remember, and put all the little slips and incongruities together, he'd gone back to Antigua and come to Tangiers. Luck had been with him, because the dogs were gone. And he'd thought Steve had been taken to jail, and I was alone in the house with one frail old woman.

And even then the danger of waiting when he knew Steve was there had been too great. He had to kill me, quickly. And Steve alone in the house with the wires cut would have to take the blame. And now the danger of waiting was too great again. He took a step toward me, and I saw his eyes resting on my arm—and I knew and thought desperately that I'd told him how to kill me. Doctor Richards and I both had told him. They'd think something had happened—I'd fainted, maybe, and hit my arm, and the ligature broke, and I just bled to death.

He came a little closer. His eyes were bright, and his face had gone white and hard and terrible. We were still talking, about what I have no idea at all, and he was still trying to make it look as if he wasn't going to do it. There was no use screaming, I knew. No one would hear me, probably, and he could easily stop my breath with his hand before the old colored woman could come, if she was still in the house and did hear. And if I tried to get up and run, I would faint, and then it would be too easy.

I just sat there. I must say something, I thought, to gain one more precious moment of time. *Oh, Tom!* I thought; *or oh, Steve! Anybody—the postman or Jim Bailey or the man bringing back the hounds!* I heard myself saying then —and why I had to say that of all things I can't imagine— "What are you going to do now you have your father's money?"

He came across the room toward me then, with quick steps, still very white-faced and bright-eyed, and I could feel the room whirl dizzily around in front of my reeling brain. And something else! There was a shout, and I could hear a door bursting in, a falling chair, a crashing table and a shot, and then a thousand tinkling falling bits of glass, and men's voices like animals, struggling, panting in hard, terrible gasps, and another shot, and then silence.

I looked out of dazed and paralyzed eyes. Alec Cartwright was lying on the floor, and Steve Heywood was getting up slowly, one hand clenched tightly around his wrist, the blood streaming out of it.

Then a horrified voice spoke from the doorway. It was Anne. "Steve! Louise! My God, not *Alec!*"

She was standing there, holding on to the frame, staring at the motionless form lying on the carpet in front of the fireplace.

"Phone Jim Bailey," Steve said. "And the doctor. Get Louise out of here. Then come and tie up my arm."

He came over to me.

"I knew I'd seen that car of his at the service station," he said. "And then I remembered seeing his face through the windshield. He came in behind us as we were pulling out."

I nodded. "I remember," I whispered.

"I'm sorry," he said.

"I'm glad," I said. "Thanks a lot."

I tried to smile.

I WAS IN THE LIBRARY across the hall. It was damp and dismal, the way rooms are that are never used and seldom opened. Anne had laid a fire and lighted it, and gone back into the kitchen to help Doctor Richards boil his instruments for the second time in less than twelve hours. Jim Bailey and a detective they'd got up from New Orleans were in the parlor. In a little while they'd be over here to talk to me about Alec.

I sat in the big green leather chair I'd pulled to the fireplace, gladder than I knew how to say that I could just tell them the facts, and that I wouldn't have to mention at all, much less try to conceal—and be fearful all the time I was concealing it—the whole story of Miss Letty and her locket, that had been so tangled through it until it was stripped to the bone. Anne's story and her mother's could stay locked in the minds of the five people —eight people now—who knew it. I wondered vaguely who the five had been. Judge Drayton and Miss Kate and Miss Letty were three. And Lawrence, because that must have been what Judge Drayton had stopped him from saying the night Cornelia had overheard them. Isaac would probably be the fifth. Lawrence was the only one I wouldn't trust, when he'd had a drink or two, I thought, if she still refused to marry him. And maybe she'd give him the plantations, and then maybe the Judge would let her marry Steve. I must suggest that to her, I thought.

Somebody turned the door knob, and I glanced back. It was Miss Rose Heywood. She had her hat on, and an old fur coat, both of which must have been in the attic for years before she dragged them out. She came in.

"I declare," she said. "I don't know what all's going on around here."

Her voice was high and querulous and vague, the way deaf people's voices get. "The mayor called me up and asked me to come to his office, and when I got there he pretended he'd never called me at all. I was so provoked."

She took off her gloves and looked around the room.

"I don't use it," she said. "It's been closed up since Minot Heywood died. I hate to come in here. I can see us all sitting around after the funeral, listening to Vidal read our grandmother's will. Minot sat there where you are. Vidal had to read it twice, and explain it over and over before he seemed to be able to understand it. Some people thought the rest of us ought to contest it, but I wouldn't join them, and next to Minot I'd had the most to contend with. I get along very nicely, with tourists and showing people the house. I show them this room and the parlor. I showed that first lady that got killed around that same day. She kept asking questions about the portrait of my grandmother in the parlor. She said she was sure she'd seen the locket she had around her neck somewhere or other."

"What's happened to it?" I asked. I tried to ask it as calmly as possible.

"It's in the other room. Or do you mean the locket? I don't know what's happened to that. Grandmother always thought one of the servants took it. When she was angry at Minot she used to accuse him of stealing it and pawning it. Well, I hope you're going to be comfortable. Who are all these people? Jim Bailey, why aren't you out sheriffing?"

Jim got her out eventually. I looked again at the man from New Orleans. I was very glad he hadn't come that morning. The powder on the floor upstairs and on Steve's shoes and coat and on my slippers wouldn't have escaped him very long. Then Steve and Anne came in, too, Steve with his arm in a sling, and Anne looking at him with anxious eyes. They didn't get very far away from each other.

I told them everything that had happened, just leaving out his question about the locket, and the way he'd looked at me then that had made me suddenly realize all the rest of it.

"That car has a special motor," the man from New Orleans said. "He could make it to Natchez in less than four hours, if he didn't get pinched for speeding, and that was a chance he had to take. I'll check up at the airport about that plane."

He reached in his pocket. "Is this her watch?"

He held Cornelia's diamond wrist watch out. I nodded.

"It was in his pocket. How was he off for money? All he had was a couple of dollars and two pawn tickets in his billfold."

"She was very close," I said. "It was his father's money. If it had just been Cornelia—Mrs. Cartwright—well, she's never been very kind to him."

They left after a while, the man from New Orleans and Jim Bailey, and Steve closed the door behind them and came back into the room. I turned my chair and sat looking at the fire. It was dying slowly, unable to make any headway against the accumulated dampness of the chimney flue. Steve and Anne came over, and Anne leaned down and kissed me.

"Good-by, Louise," she said softly. "I've got to go now."

"I'll come with you," Steve said.

She shook her head. "No—it—it just makes it harder. We'll do as we said, and then, some day—if you still love me—"

She looked up at him and smiled, her eyes glittering with tears.

"I'll come to the door then," Steve said.

"Good-by, Louise."

"Good-by, Anne," I said.

They started slowly to the door, Steve's good hand gripping hers.

"Give me my jacket there before you go, will you, Anne?" I said.

She picked it up off the horsehair settee where I'd laid it. She must have been blinded with tears, because she got it by the bottom, and as she held it up there was a thud on the carpet, and Miss Letty's locket lay there, wide open as the clasp had unloosed. And for the second time I saw that little oblong bit of folded paper.

We looked at it, all three of us, quite motionless. Then Steve bent down. I realized as he did that he was the only one of us who had no sense of the inviolability of its contents. I'd told him about Miss Letty flying into a rage with Cornelia, but so many things had happened since that any importance that it may have had must have quite disappeared.

He picked up the little piece of paper, opened it out, and looked down at it. He stood there for an instant, turned into a bronze statue. Then, very slowly, he handed it over to Anne. Her eyes were searching his face, not knowing whether it was a new blow of some kind, not being sure she wanted it to fall.

"Read it," he said.

She took it from him.

"—'David Norman 22, Bella Sykes 18,' " she read aloud. " 'Allen Smith 28, Ella Bachelor 29. Minot Heywood 32, Laetitia Drayton 27'— Oh, Steve! Then they were—they *were* married! Oh, Steve, Steve!"

Miss Letty must be fifty now, I thought. *That means it was the year he went to war. Anne was born after he'd come back.*

"Be careful of your arm," I heard her whisper, and Steve laughed.

"I don't care about my arm."

"Be careful of Miss Letty's locket," I said practically.

He grinned, reached down and picked it up off the floor. "What's this?" he said. "Stop crying, Anne. You can't get out of it now, no matter what happens."

"I don't want to get out of it!"

"Then let's read this, too."

"What is it?" I demanded. I got up and went over to them. In his hand he had a thin sheet of air mail paper that had been folded a dozen times and pressed into the cavity of the locket, facing the picture of a man in khaki. It was a badly faded likeness, cut from a passport picture that had probably been made for army identification. Slipped in beside the picture was a tiny snapshot of a baby.

"You've changed a lot, thank God, Anne," Steve said, looking at it. She took the locket from him and unfolded the piece of paper.

"Read it," she said. "What's that date?"

" 'December 2, 1935,' " Steve read.

"That was the day Mr. Minot died," she said quickly. "He must have—oh, read it, Steve. What did he say to her? He did write it, didn't he? Look on the back."

He turned it over. *Until four days from now, my dearest,* I could see. *All my love as always.*

It was signed, *Minot*. There was a postscript, but he turned the letter over before I could read it.

The folds were dark and frayed, and the whole had been blurred with tears. I probably don't remember it word for word, but this is the way I recall it, as Steve read it, picking out the words and going back to make them sound coherent, every once in a while.

" 'My dearest, I'm coming to you at last. I've always been with you in my heart. When Vidal read her will today, and I realized it meant we'd not only be together again after the years she'd kept us apart, but that we'd have a chance to do all the things we dreamed of doing, I couldn't feel bitter toward her any more. And of course, I'd been a coward. I should have broken away the day you told me. If you'd told me before you brought her back, I believe that I'm man enough to have done it in spite of her, and in spite of Kate. She had been happy, and maybe you were right in thinking it made up our debt to her, letting her have the child. Maybe I couldn't have made a living for us all. I'm not proud of my life, but I'm proud of your love, and of Anne. And now I'm coming. My love, my wife—we are together at last. Until four days from now, my dearest, all my love as always.' "

The fire sizzled out on the hearth. It was the only sound in the room for a long time. Then I said, "What's the rest of it?"

Steve read the postscript.

" 'Kate has just phoned. She's coming across the bayou tonight at nine o'clock. It's the only time since I realized it was you I loved that I've been glad to see her. I'll tell her everything. We'll both be glad she finally knows. Good-by for now, my dear wife. Minot.' "

Anne sat there staring in front of her a long time.

"He never got the chance to tell her," she said at last. "She must have come too late. Oh, what a difference it would have made. Aunt—my mother could have come back and lived with us then."

Steve looked at me. Neither of us said anything.

"She must have been just a little late coming through the bayou," Anne said. She was talking almost as if she were in a dream. "Just such a few minutes, to make so much difference in everybody's life."

She got up, went over to the desk, and pulled open the drawer. It was filled with dusty papers and old plantation accounts. She picked something up and came back to us. It was a thick, old-fashioned watch on a heavy gold chain. She held it out to me. The crystal was cracked in a hundred splintered facets.

"Miss Rose put it there," she said to Steve, "to keep until you came. We put it there together, before his funeral.

I sneaked through the bayou to say good-by to him, but she wouldn't let me see him. You see—it broke when he fell. Poor Aunt Kate—if she'd only known. She grieved for him for days."

I looked down at the watch, and saw that the hands were standing at seven minutes past nine. Steve took it gently out of her hands and put it back in the desk drawer. Then he came back and took her in his arms, holding her tightly against him, kissing the top of her shining head. After a moment our gaze met across the room. He shook his head slowly, and I nodded mine in return.

"I love you, Anne," he whispered softly.